Come Autumn

Bedside Books
An imprint of American Book Publishing
5442 So. 900 East, #146
Salt Lake City, UT 84117-7204

www.american-book.com
Printed in the United States of America on acid-free paper.

Come Autumn
Designed by Julia Stilchen, design@american-book.com

Publisher's Note: This is a work of fiction. Names, characters, places, and incidents either are the product of the author's imagination, or are used fictitiously, and any resemblance to actual persons, living or dead, events, or locales is entirely coincidental.

ISBN-13: 978-1-58982-577-2
ISBN-10: 1-58982-577-2

Kern, Nannette Monson, Come Autumn

Come Autumn

Nannette Monson Kern

Dedication

This one's for you, Daddy.

Foreword

Ecclesiastes 3:1-8
To every thing there is a season, and a time to every purpose under the heaven: A time to be born and a time to die . . . A time to weep and a time to laugh, a time to mourn and a time to dance . . . A time to love . . .

Chapter I

Margie Nelson fell in love with her cousin, Richard, when she was six years old; he was fourteen. She didn't perceive him as overtly handsome–though exceedingly masculine, to be sure. Tall with dark hair, brown eyes, and a muscular body, he possessed a certain charisma and joie de vivre that she could not resist. Also the fact that he treated her with respect and consideration–something beyond the comprehension of her less mature kinsmen–greatly enhanced his appeal.

Margie's mother, Grace, and Richard's mother, Vera, were uncommonly devoted to each other and fortunately lived in close enough proximity to enjoy a steadfast relationship. They spent most of their leisurely hours united, and along with a third sister, Leone, often gathered their families for a pleasant evening together.

It was a warm Friday night in the middle of May with the family all assembled at Vera's home for dinner. The meal was over and the sisters were in the kitchen cleaning up; the others had retired to the living room. Margie's only sibling, Jack–four years her senior–was seated on the floor with Aunt Leone's three offspring, the four of them occupied with Richard's stereoscope and snickering over several explicit photographs from the *National Geographic* magazine. Jon, the oldest of Leone's children, was ten–the same age as Jack–and her twins, Danny and Mark, were one year younger. Consequently, these four boys were inseparable and exclusive, which invariably left Richard, the only child of a single mom (Aunt Vera had been divorced for several years), and Margie as the "odd men out." They didn't seem to mind.

Margie's dad, George, was relaxing at one end of the chintz-covered sofa, visiting with Leone's husband, Ted, who occupied the opposite end. Grandma was sitting quietly in a comfortable overstuffed chair, enjoying the sounds of her family. Margie was curled up at her feet, soothed by her loving aura and the drone of her daddy's voice.

Richard seated himself at the piano and began conjuring up unstructured improvisations, for which he had an amazing proclivity. Margie was immediately drawn to the instrument, where she timidly climbed up next to him on the bench, mesmerized as always by his music–and by Richard.

"Hey, Kiddo," he said, glancing in her direction, "anything you'd like to hear?"

She shrugged. "I don't know."

Richard kept on for a few moments with his musical trivia then turned and winked at his young cousin. "How about this one?" he asked.

Margie recognized the tune, knew the words, and needed no encouragement to join in. Singing was her passion, even at that tender age. In a high, clear voice she began:

I'll be loving you
Always,
With a love that's true
Always.

When the things you've planned
Need a helping hand,
I will understand
Always, always.
Days may not be fair
Always;
That's when I'll be there
Always-
Not for just an hour,
Not for just a day,
Not for just a year,
But always.

Richard continued playing but turned a grinning face to Margie. "So, will you?" he asked.

Margie looked up at him in bewilderment. "Will I what?" she asked.

"Will you love me always?" he replied.

Margie tittered shyly, ducking her head. "Yes," she said quietly.

"Even when you grow up and have all kinds of boys chasing after you?" he teased. She nodded her head.

"Well, when that time comes, if ever any of those boys don't treat you right, you just come to me and I promise you there'll be 'Slaughter on Tenth Avenue!'"

Margie smiled up at him, not completely taking in the meaning of his words but understanding, nevertheless, that he had just appointed himself her guardian and protector. "Okay," she said, her heart swelling to unnatural proportions.

"So, what now?"

Margie shrugged again. "I don't care. Just make something up." She loved the way that he could almost make the piano talk to her. Sometimes it painted pictures in her mind that made her laugh; other times she wanted to cry. Either way, she relished the experience. Richard blissfully played on, glancing at her from time to time, smiling in amusement, and doubtless pleasure, at her obvious adulation.

It's a little more difficult to pinpoint the exact moment when Richard's feelings toward his little cousin began to deepen. It may be that he had always been slightly smitten. She was, after all, a charmer from the get-go, with her golden curls and shy ways. And he was not oblivious to the fact that she believed him to be approaching omniscience–was there ever a man or boy created who could possibly resist such absolute veneration?

On the first Sunday morning in December of that year, the Nelson family was attending church, as was their custom. Just before the meeting began, the bishop stood and solemnly announced that Japanese planes had attacked Pearl Harbor early that morning. The toll in Navy battleships and human lives was inestimable, and as a result, war had been declared by President Roosevelt.

Margie had no concept of the magnitude of his statement–she didn't even know the location of Pearl Harbor, assuming it to be in some remote area of Europe–but was struck by the shock and alarm that swept over the congregation. She sensed her mother's body stiffening at her side and looked to her for some indication that all was well, but Grace's face reflected something close to terror, and Margie felt an unidentifiable anxiety rising within her. "Mama?" she murmured tentatively.

Grace looked down at her young daughter and placed an arm around her shoulders in an attempt to reassure her, then bent her head down close to Margie's ear. "Shhh, it's okay," she whispered. "We'll talk about it when we get home."

A major transformation was about to take place in the United States. The family unit would never again function in a normal way. Women would leave their homes to become factory workers, while their husbands and sons were sacrificed for the welfare of the country. It was a frightening prospect, and Grace and her sisters counted it as a great blessing that none of their men qualified for the armed services; they were either too young or too old.

Because Margie's father was the vice president and general manager of a large aircraft corporation, his normal interaction with the Air Force was immediately escalated. Commutes to Washington D.C., though always part of his job, now became almost a monthly necessity. Margie hated his frequent, prolonged absences, but other than that, noticed little disruption in her safe world. There were, of course, the nightly radio broadcasts that kept her parents glued to their receivers, and the occasional piercing sound of nearby sirens. While always alarming, the scream of the sirens was usually short lived and initiated mostly as a drill to insure that all would be prepared in the unlikely event of an enemy air attack.

George had volunteered as an air-raid warden, and when an alert was sounded, he walked the streets of their neighborhood to check for any sign of forbidden light peeking around the mandatory blackout curtains. Margie was always fearful during these exercises, imagining all of the terror that would be wrought by the actual dropping of an enemy bomb and envisioning her dear daddy being shot down in the street by a barrage of foreign bullets. The movies were full of such scenes occurring in other parts of the world, and Margie worried that the horror might eventually infiltrate her own neighborhood.

One such drill occurred on a night when the extended family had congregated at the Nelson home for one of their usual get-togethers. Abruptly, the warning sirens shattered the tranquility of the evening. George immediately and silently grabbed his dark jacket from the entry closet and departed the house. The sisters went from room to room, hurriedly turning off lights as the rest of the family gathered in the living room in sober anticipation. Margie sat on the floor with her back against the wall, her arms clutching her knees firmly to her chest, her eyes wide with fear.

"You scared, Kiddo?" Richard had lowered himself to the floor close beside her, and she was straightaway comforted by his nearness.

Margie nodded in the darkness. "Yeah," she admitted. "A little bit."

"There's nothing to be afraid of," he consoled her. "This is just a practice thing, like your fire drills at school. You know? There aren't really any enemy planes flying around overhead."

"But they might come," she argued.

"Nah. This war will never be fought in the United States." Richard wasn't certain whether his proclamation was more for his assurance or for Margie's. In all honesty, he had concerns of his own, but he wasn't about to expose them to his frightened young cousin.

"How do you know?" she asked.

That was the trouble. He didn't know; he only hoped. So he merely smiled at her with as much confidence as he could muster. "Trust me," he said. "I understand these things."

"You think we'll always be safe here?"

"I think you shouldn't worry your pretty little head about it."

Margie was pacified, more perhaps because Richard had called her pretty than by his promise of safety. But with the sounding of the "all clear," everything returned to normal and she felt secure again. Richard was right, as always. There really was nothing for her to worry about.

Throughout the duration of the war, Margie listened as her parents and their friends commiserated over the shortage of rubber for automobile tires and the aggravation of needing stamps for gasoline and food items; nevertheless, George had connections whereby he could obtain certain commodities which were, for all intents and purposes, nonexistent for the less privileged. The Nelson family sacrificed little in the way of creature comforts–Grace was still able to wear silk hose and have cream on her breakfast cereal–and in most respects, life continued on in normal fashion.

On the morning after Margie's seventh birthday, her mother called her to the telephone. "It's Richard," she said. "He wants to know if you'd like to go with him and your Aunt Vera to Big Bear for the weekend. I think Grandma's going along, too."

Margie excitedly took the phone. "Richard? Do you really want me to go?"

"I wouldn't ask if I didn't. Can you be ready in an hour?" he asked.

"Mom?" Margie asked, turning to Grace. "Can I be ready in an hour?"

Grace smiled. "I think we can manage that."

"Okay," Margie spoke again into the phone. "Are you going to pick me up?"

"Of course," Richard replied. "What kind of a cheap date do you think I am?"

Margie giggled. "You're not a date! You're my cousin!"

"Can't I be both?"

"Cousins don't date!" she said, with all the wisdom of a

barely seven –year old.

"Don't be too sure, Kiddo! I'll see you in about an hour."

Margie was packed and waiting by the time Richard, Aunt Vera, and Grandma pulled into the driveway. Richard tossed her bag into the trunk of the car, and he and Margie climbed into the back seat. The two young people kept themselves entertained, singing and playing travel games, until they arrived at their destination. Richard's singing voice was strictly utilitarian, the only thing about him, as far as Margie could tell, that wasn't perfection itself. His ear was true and he sang on key, but that was the extent of his vocal abilities. However, he was a good sport and performed the songs with gusto, which made Margie laugh in delight. How she adored this fascinating young man at her side!

Vera pulled up in front of their rented two-room cabin, and Richard helped her unload the bags while Grandma busied herself opening every available window to welcome in the fresh mountain air. As soon as the luggage was inside, Richard winked at Margie and asked, "Anybody want to take a swim with me?"

"Okay," was her eager reply; she was always ready for a water frolic.

"Get your suit on, and let's go," ordered Richard.

Margie didn't have to be told twice. She ran into the small bedroom and hastily donned swimming attire and grabbed a towel. Richard was waiting in front of the cabin when she came out–he had worn trunks under his clothes to facilitate a quick easy change.

"I'll race you to the water," he challenged.

"That's no fair. You're bigger than I am!" she complained, stuffing her hair into a bathing cap.

"Okay, then, how about this?" He grabbed her up in his

arms and sprinted to the edge of the lake, Margie laughing uncontrollably all the way. "It's a tie!" he announced, placing her firmly on the ground. Margie's giggles gradually subsided as she tugged down on her suit where it had hiked up in the back and carefully laid out her towel, all the while surveying the beckoning water. "Last one in is a sissy!" Richard didn't wait for an even start but immediately splashed into the water with Margie following a few yards behind.

"Ooh, it's cold!" she shrieked.

"Of course it is," he laughed, turning toward her. "Water's always cold in the mountains."

"How come?" she asked, hugging herself and shivering.

Richard waded back to explain, "Because it comes from melting snow." He dipped his hands into the lake and playfully began dousing her. Margie ineffectually tried to reciprocate, simultaneously attempting to avoid his onslaught and squealing for him to stop. Finding herself at an insurmountable disadvantage she good naturedly sloshed her way back to the shore and sat down, shivering. Richard followed with a grin on his face. "In spite of the fact that we're in sunny California," he went on assiduously as he smoothed out his towel and plopped down beside her, "this lake is fed completely from snow melt. In fact, in the northern part of the state, there are even mountains with glaciers on 'em."

Margie's brow wrinkled in concentration. "What's a glacier?" she asked.

Richard leaned back on his elbows, stretching his legs out in front of him. "It's a big chunk of ice that covers the whole top of the mountain and never melts," he elucidated.

"Not even in the summertime?"

"Nope."

She was incredulous, but never doubted for a moment that

Richard knew what he was talking about. He was to her the consummate guru, and she was gratified that he never complained about taking the time to teach her.

That night, the four of them sat around a campfire under an umbrella of stars so bright and close that Margie imagined herself reaching out and plucking one from the sky. Richard strummed his guitar while he and Margie sang the songs that were popular in their mothers' heyday, songs that had somehow trickled down to become a part of this younger generation's musical repertoire. Margie wanted it never to end. She could happily spend the rest of her life singing to Richard's accompaniment.

Chapter II

Margie adored her grandma and enjoyed immensely the frequent sleepovers at her small apartment. They baked cookies, played paper dolls (Grandma sat with Margie on the floor and produced the voice and animation for one of the cardboard characters while Margie did the same for the other), and listened to their favorite radio programs, *The Great Gildersleeve* heading the list. Then Grandma would tuck her in on the couch and read to her until one of them fell asleep, usually Grandma. The next morning, there would be bacon and waffles with lots of rationed butter (compliments of George) and maple syrup, accompanied by a large glass of milk. It was Margie's favorite breakfast, consumed while in their pajamas as they listened to *Arthur Godfrey's Breakfast Club*. Then, as they washed the dishes, Grandma would tell Margie stories–the same ones, over and over, of which Margie never tired–about her childhood.

"Tell me about my mama," was a frequent request from Margie.

"Your mama was the belle of the ball until your handsome daddy swept her off her feet and claimed her heart. From the time she was about your age, she loved to dance. I'd take my three little girls to all the town dances with me, and they'd hold hands and twirl around the floor together–so cute!" Grandma pulled her hands out of the dishwater and rested them on the edge of the sink as she gazed out of the window, seeing not the grey stucco wall of her neighbor's apartment, but three darling little girls in frilly blue dresses, laughing delightedly together.

Then, forcing her thoughts back to the present and returning to the job at hand, she continued, "I remember once, when your mama was a teenager (though we didn't call them that then; they were simply 'the youngsters'). She and Vera and Leone used to love to look through the fashion magazines to see what the latest styles were in New York. Then we'd make patterns and sew them up. My girls were the best-dressed girls in all of Wyoming! And, oh, did the old biddies like to wag their tongues over our little family and their 'modern' ways.

"Anyway, your mama had spotted a dress in one of those magazines and fallen in love with it. So, of course, I made it for her to wear to the school dance. She looked so pretty! Trouble was, she had only been gone that night for a very short time before she came bounding back through the door, throwing herself on the bed and weeping as if her heart would break!"

"What happened?" Margie's toweled hand halted in the middle of its swirl over the top of a dinner plate.

"Well, you know those old biddies I told you about? Seems they didn't approve of the style of your mama's dress. One shoulder was bare, you see, and they made sure your mama heard them discussing her 'unseemly' attire and declaring that a widow lady like myself should have more sense than to allow her daughter to appear in public dressed like a hussy! I've never really been able to figure out why my being a widow should give me any particular kind of sense, but I just felt awful when your mama told me what had happened. I'd only wanted her to look nice, and she did! She looked beautiful! Your daddy thought so, too; he was the one who took her to the dance that night. She thought she'd never be able to face him again after that, being so embarrassed and all. But he smoothed it over, and now they're living happily ever after." Grandma smiled and winked at her use of the platitude.

Margie resumed rubbing the already dry plate, averted her eyes, and asked, "Did cousins ever get married back in the olden days, Grandma?"

"Now, where did that question come from?"

Margie shrugged. "I just wondered."

"Well, yes. Sometimes. We lived in a smaller world back then. Young people didn't have the chance to meet a lot of folks who weren't related to them. But why do you ask?"

"No reason." Grandma was curious, but Margie refused to explain.

Later that week, on a sunny Saturday, the three families took a picnic lunch to Griffith Park, a favorite retreat. The sisters spread blankets on the ground and retrieved the lunch from the cooler, chattering together as usual, while the four boys climbed trees and played tag. George and Ted were taking turns with the crank on the ice cream freezer, discussing the progress of the war and speculating over its probable progression and conclusion. Richard and Margie sat with their backs against a large tree while Richard entertained his young cousin with a Jew's harp, which he had brought along specifically for that purpose. Though the sound emanating from the small instrument was not the most pleasing to the ear, Margie was intrigued.

"Why's it called a 'Jew's harp'?" she asked inquisitively.

Richard pursed his lips. "No one really knows," he said. "Lots of theories, though; a few are quite interesting. Some people think it was originally called a 'juice' harp because when you're first learning how to play it, you slobber a lot."

Margie laughed and Richard joined in. "I didn't say it was true," he disclaimed, "just one of the theories. Whatever it's called, it's been around for a long time, maybe even as early as the third century B.C., so it's hard to say how it got its name." Richard resumed playing, and Margie sat close by his side fascinated and, as always, enamored.

Grandma invariably came along on the family outings, never had much to say, but was a comforting presence. She silently considered Richard and Margie as they sat side by side, clearly reveling in each other's company, and she suddenly remembered Margie's earlier question about cousins marrying. Realization dawned. It was clear at this point that Margie was in love, but she was just a child, and chances were that she'd outgrow the infatuation. Richard, on the other hand, was displaying a serious attraction toward his young cousin and was old enough that his heart could be severely broken. Grandma hoped that this would not be the case. Right now, Margie worshiped the ground he walked on, but what about ten years from now after she'd had time to outgrow her childhood fantasies? Would she still be enchanted? Grandma felt a special affection for these two and didn't want either of them to be hurt; she would be a careful observer.

It was a perfect day to be outdoors, not a cloud in the sky, the temperature around eighty degrees, typical southern California weather. After feasting on cold chicken shish-ka-bobs (Grace's specialty), potato salad, and homemade ice cream, they all helped gather up the trash and place it in nearby garbage containers. The adults returned to relax on the blankets, feeling the lassitude induced by full stomachs.

Richard beckoned to Margie. "Come take a walk with me," he invited. She eagerly complied and, as they wove their way among the trees, he asked about her favorite school subjects, the books she was reading, and the music she was studying; he loved to watch as she effervesced over things about which she was passionate.

"Has anyone ever told you that you have a million dollar smile?" Richard asked, his own mouth curving upward in delight at his cousin's exuberance.

Margie dropped her eyes and shook her head.

"You do, you know."

Margie pressed her lips together, embarrassed now to display any teeth and doubtful of the verity of his compliment. "Jack calls me 'bucktooth,'" she stated abjectly.

"Ah, Kiddo, don't let him fool you. That's just big brother talk. Besides, a smile is more than just a matter of teeth; it's the way it makes your eyes sparkle and your face come alive. It's just one of the many remarkable things about you," Richard declared firmly, amused at the flush it brought to Margie's cheeks. "Now you're supposed to tell me how terrific I am," he teased.

Margie laughed softly, then raised her eyes to his. "You really are," she admitted shyly.

Richard slung his arm across her shoulders and gave her a brief tug. "That's my girl," he chuckled, as Margie beamed with pleasure. "Guess we'd better head back," he said reluctantly. "They're probably wondering about us."

As they neared their picnic spot, they became aware that the adults were speaking intently to each other in quiet tones, an indication to Margie that their conversation was private and therefore undoubtedly of great interest to her. Had she been alone, she might have slowed her steps to create a longer listening time before being discovered. With Richard at her side, however, she felt the need to curtail her impulses, so she was only able to glean a small tidbit from their communication, one that seemed of little importance to her. Grace was saying, "I'm not sure we should lightly dismiss this. If it becomes serious, we may have to consider telling them." Vera was shaking her head vehemently and about to respond when George spied the two young people returning from their walk.

In a booming voice, he cut off Vera's reply by announcing, "Here they are," and then quickly suggesting, "How about a visit to the observatory?"

Margie was spellbound by the ceiling full of "stars" and Richard, sitting next to her, patiently pointed out and explained the different constellations, introducing her to the Big and Little Dippers, Orion, the North Star, the Milky Way, and many others. While the idea of endless space and countless celestial bodies was too vast for Margie to conceptualize, her cousin was able, as usual, to expound on the subject with ease. Margie's rapt attention was divided between the heavenly display and her cousin's expressive countenance. She covertly observed his manly profile. His wisdom astounded her; his talent enraptured her; his attentions delighted her.

Chapter III

Richard began high school in the fall, and the school band profited immensely from his membership. He performed admirably on the trumpet, thus inspiring his fellow musicians to higher levels of proficiency. He also participated in track and field events, and demonstrated, as well, an uncommon propensity for football. Every endeavor he pursued earned Margie's admiration; it seemed that he could fail at nothing. She kept telling herself that nobody's perfect, yet Richard continuously refuted the maxim.

The following year, as a sophomore, he earned the coveted position of quarterback and was not only Margie's hero, but the idol of every girl at Westchester High. He dated a few of his adoring fans but quickly tired of their vacuous companionship. The school undoubtedly harbored plenty of females who were not mentally challenged, but it seemed that those whom Richard regarded as physically attractive possessed minimal cognitive skills. In his opinion, Margie had more brains, aptitude, and motivation than all of them put together, and he preferred her company, hands down.

Margie was always delighted when Richard unexpectedly dropped by, and, much as she loved Nancy Drew, she willingly forsook an evening with her favorite girl detective to spend a few hours with her favorite boy cousin. They worked puzzles and played games; Margie was an adequate and competitive opponent. They talked of Margie's juvenile concerns, Richard's future aspirations, and even what kind of mystery Nancy Drew was currently solving. It was an uncommon and soul-satisfying relationship for both of them, as Richard endlessly explained, exhibited, and extolled in answer to Margie's insatiable curiosity. Of course, they spent countless hours together at the piano, singing and playing, laughing, and occasionally becoming serious as their eyes would meet, unavoidably betraying the feelings which they were reluctant to acknowledge. Margie would then quickly turn away, unable to interpret the message in Richard's eyes but only aware that her own might be too revealing. And Richard would instantly lighten the mood with some keyboard inanity, inspiring more chuckles from Margie; the moment would pass almost unnoticed.

Richard's buddies may have considered his attraction toward his cousin to be an unnatural obsession, and anyone but he might easily have been ostracized from their friendship over what they viewed as questionable behavior, but Richard's very normal and macho conduct when he was with "the guys" quelled their misgivings. If he preferred his cousin to all of the "hot chicks" at school, their only conclusion was that she must be something indeed!

George and Grace (they were amused by the fact that they shared names with the famous radio duo) were avid moviegoers and didn't hesitate to take their children out on a school night–sometimes two or three times a week–as long as their homework was completed beforehand. They never bothered to inquire as to show times; they just left home whenever they got ready, often arriving in the middle of the movie. In those innocent days, plots were vastly different from the convoluted themes of later years; it was relatively easy to deduce what events had already transpired, as well as what was to come!

With the advent of the war, the aspect had changed–the leading man wore a uniform–but the theme remained with little variation: boy meets girl, boy loses girl, boy gets girl. A few exceptions were the writings of Ernie Pyle, a well-known war correspondent, whose experiences had been aptly captured on the big screen. One such, *The Story of GI Joe*, was nominated for several Academy Awards. Whether action filled or romantic, sorrowful or hilarious, it was all the same to the Nelsons: good entertainment and well worth the twenty-five cent admission charge.

If Richard happened to come by on an evening when the family planned to go out, he simply hopped into their car and went with them. As far as Margie was concerned, having him along made the outing remarkable, rather than merely pleasurable.

"What're we going to see?" he asked on one of these occasions, as the car pulled out of the Nelson's driveway.

"*Thirty Seconds Over Tokyo*," was Margie's eager response.

"Is that the one that's a true story?"

"That's the one," confirmed George.

Richard turned to Margie and said, "You like true stories."

She nodded her head. "They're my favorite."

"I have to agree with you there, Kiddo. Much more fun when it's real."

The movie had everything: action, romance, pathos, and Van Johnson. The story left Margie with an indefinable yearning, which rendered her mute throughout much of the ride home. She and Richard were the lone occupants of the back seat. After several miles of silence, Richard became uneasy with Margie's lassitude and quietly began to prod her out of her reverie.

"How would you feel," he asked softly, "if I went to war and came home with my leg amputated like the guy in the movie?"

Margie snapped to attention, intrigued by the idea. She would never want Richard to be hurt, of course, but it would be terribly romantic. "Do you think the war will last long enough for you to get drafted?"

Richard shrugged. "Maybe. It's already lasted longer than anyone thought it would." He grinned at her. "So, would you still love me?"

Margie giggled, hoping that would suffice for an answer, but Richard wasn't so easily appeased. "Well?"

She looked out the side window, away from Richard, and nodded, "Uh-huh."

Chapter IV

The war, for all intents and purposes, came to its conclusion during the summer of the following year. A few days after atomic bombs destroyed Hiroshima and Nagasaki, Japan surrendered to the United States. Unmindful of the horror thus brought to bear upon the Japanese people, be they innocent or otherwise, America breathed a collective sigh of relief. After an interminable three and a half years, her patriot sons would at long last return home in triumph.

But their homecoming would force the nation once again into a state of flux; the supposition that life could automatically return to prewar conditions was a pipe dream. Jobs that soldiers had left behind were now being held down by women, and the women, who enjoyed their newly recognized value, were not so willing to give it up. Again, the Nelsons were relatively untouched by the turmoil that surrounded them. The war and its aftermath had little effect on their private world.

Nevertheless, Grace and her sisters were grateful to see the end of the conflict. Vera, especially, counted her blessings. Richard was nearing draft age, and the thought of her only son being called upon to risk his life in battle was more than she could bear. She basked in the knowledge that he could now complete his last year in high school with no worries over impending service in the armed forces.

The head football coach at Westchester High had taken an instant liking to Richard, as had most of his teachers, and by the time the young athlete was a senior, he was riding along as the single passenger in Coach Billings' private car to events held away from their home field.

"So, what kind of plans do you have after you graduate from high school?" Billings asked on one such out-of-town excursion. "I assume you'll go on to college. Do you have any intentions of turning professional?"

"Mmm, well, I like sports but hadn't really considered it as a career," answered Richard. "Basically, I'm a musician. I'm also smart enough to know that it's pretty hard to make a living blowing a horn. So, I'm not sure yet what direction I'll take."

"You might think about pro ball," Billings said. "You've got the talent."

"I don't know. Just doesn't seem right for me. As far as my future plans, I think I'd like to see something of the world before I settle down. And that's not going to happen any time soon–settling down, I mean."

"Don't be too sure," replied Billings, who not only enjoyed his role as coach, but also took pleasure in counseling "his boys" in personal matters. "When you meet the right person, it can happen fast."

Richard gave a wry chortle and shook his head. He would have felt foolish admitting to his coach that he was infatuated with a ten year old, and his first cousin at that! He was only beginning to acknowledge the fact to himself.

In the wee hours of a Saturday morning, three months before Richard was to graduate from high school, Grace received a hysterical phone call from Vera. "Grace, I don't know what to do. Richard's been in horrible pain all night, and I don't know what's wrong with him!

"You'd better call the doctor," Grace advised. "Don't worry about the cost. Then call me right back." Grace was well aware that Vera had no health insurance and therefore hesitated to seek a physician's counsel, preferring home remedies to costly office or hospital visits. Vera was also very independent and seldom asked even her own sisters for advice or help; Richard's condition must be grievous indeed.

The family physician insisted that Vera take her son immediately to the hospital where he would join them. Vera quickly redialed Grace's number, the first ring not even completed before the other end was picked up. "I'll meet you there," Grace assured her without a second thought. Then, as she hung up the phone, she realized that that presented a problem. Jack had spent the night at Leone's with his cousins, and George was out of town. She was reluctant to leave Margie at home all alone; there was no alternative but to bring her daughter with her. She gently awakened an ill-tempered Margie, urged her into her clothes, and led her by the hand to the front seat of the car.

"Where are we going?" Margie murmured crossly, curling up in the seat, sleepy eyes again closed.

"Richard's not feeling well, and Aunt Vera's taking him to the hospital. We're going to meet them there."

Margie jolted to awareness. "What's the matter with him?"

"I'm not sure."

"Is it bad?"

Grace hesitated. She didn't want to frighten Margie, but on the other hand, perhaps she should prepare her for the worst. "It might be pretty bad," she finally admitted.

Margie's eyes filled. "Is he going to die?" If Richard died, she would die as well. There would no longer be any desire or purpose for her existence. She had heard of people passing away simply because they had lost the will to live.

Again Grace didn't know how to answer. "We'll have to trust that the doctor will take care of whatever's wrong."

Richard's illness proved to be an advanced case of appendicitis, and by the time that Grace and Margie arrived at the hospital, he had already been rushed into surgery. Vera was pacing the floor of the waiting room in a state of near hysterics and welcomed her sister with open arms. The two women sat together on the only available sofa and silently held hands, with Margie snuggled up next to her mother, as they anxiously awaited the doctor's report.

After what seemed an eternity, the nurse showed them into a small interview room where the surgeon joined them. "We caught it in time, barely," he said. "You came mighty close to losing that boy. An hour later and ..." The doctor slowly shook his head. "We may not have been so lucky. He'll be in recovery for awhile before you can see him. The nurse'll call you. He should be able to go home in a couple of days. Do you have any questions?" There were none.

Then came more waiting, but at least with easier minds and calmer hearts. Finally, a different nurse appeared and ushered the women into Richard's room, surreptitiously allowing Margie to accompany them after checking the halls for the presence of disapproving personnel. "It's against hospital rules to allow children into the patients' rooms," she acknowledged conspiratorially. "But as long as she doesn't stay too long and is quiet, I'll allow it." She was, from all indications, unworried about possible repercussions. But her tough exterior softened as she observed the little girl's distress.

"Don't you worry, Honey, he's gonna be okay. Is he your brother?"

Margie simply shook her head, too disquieted to find her voice.

"They're cousins," Grace enlightened the nurse, as Vera hastened to Richard's side, anxious to reassure herself that he had indeed survived. Worry lines creased her brow as she searched his beloved face for some sign of awareness, then leaned over and gently brushed the hair from his forehead. Grace stood at his foot, holding Margie's hand. She could sense that her daughter was frightened by the pale, still form occupying the bed.

"He's still groggy from the anesthesia," the nurse explained to Margie, "but you can talk to him for just a minute." She then informed the two women, "I'll be at the nurses' station if you need me. Try not to stay too long. We'll take good care of him."

Margie approached the seemingly lifeless personage with trepidation. "Richard?" Then, when there was no response, a little louder, "Richard?"

The inert body stirred, the eyelids lifted slightly, and a husky voice replied, "Hey, Kiddo, what are you doing here?"

Margie sighed, her distress easing, "I thought you were gonna die!"

"Nah," he forced the semblance of a smile, "you can't get rid of me that easy."

Until now, Margie had been too frightened to cry, but with this very typical utterance from her most esteemed cousin, she laid her cheek against the covers and wept from sheer relief, Richard's hand coming to rest on her head.

Chapter V

By June, Richard was back on his feet, had made up his school work, and was able to graduate with his class. The Nelsons, along with Leone's family, Grandma and, of course, Vera, attended the commencement ceremony, but they had barely connected with Richard afterwards before he was nabbed by his merry-making friends, who had a big celebration planned at a local restaurant. Margie was disappointed; she was still too young to understand the significance of a graduation party, nor why it was so important to spend the evening with one's buddies rather than with family. With a heavy heart and a silent tongue, she unwillingly rode home with her parents.

The next morning, Vera appeared at the Nelson home, a worried look on her face. She and Grace went into the den to talk, but before the door was closed, Margie, from her bedroom, heard Vera exclaim, "Richard came home last night with alcohol on his breath."

Margie was stunned. It couldn't be true; Richard would never do that. The family was very staunch in their religion–which shunned the use of alcohol–and she had been sure that Richard was as committed to the faith as she. It was impossible to imagine that her perfect cousin would commit so gross a sin. She crept across the living room to the door that was shut against her. Unable to make out all that was said within, she did hear enough to verify the truth of Vera's initial statement.

Margie flew to her room and threw herself, face down, on her bed. She was crushed. How could he do this to her? There was no excuse for his offensive behavior; it was stupid, stupid, stupid! She never wanted to see him again!

Nevertheless, she invited him in a day later, when he showed up on her doorstep. "Hey, Kiddo," he said in his usual nonchalant way.

"Hi Richard." Her tone was glacial. "C'mon in." She turned, without waiting for him, and walked to the living room where she flounced down on the sofa.

"Gee, Kid, was it something I said?" he joked, following after and joining her on the couch.

"No," answered Margie sternly, "it was something you did."

Richard's brows drew together. "What? Why are you so mad?"

"I think you know why."

He grunted. "No, I don't think I do."

"I'm talking about graduation night."

He looked at her quizzically. "Because I went out with my friends?"

"Because of what you did when you went out with your friends." Margie's eyes began to tear.

Richard huffed. "Oh, that. How do you know about that?"

Margie shook her head slowly, infuriated that she would cry, indicating vulnerability rather than anger. "Why would you do it, Richard?" she whined. "You know it's wrong."

"Ah, Kid, it was no big deal."

"It is too a big deal!"

"Look, I just messed up a little. One time. It'll never happen again, I promise."

"Cross your heart and hope to die?"

Richard made the appropriate X with his finger across his chest and raised his hand as if to swear, while giving her a pleading look.

Margie softened a bit. "It better not because I'll never forgive you if it does."

"Never's a long time, Kid." Richard grinned sheepishly. "Do you really think you can hold out that long?" Margie fought to maintain her stern demeanor, and Richard pressed his advantage. "So, how about we kiss and make up?" Margie's eyes widened with apprehension, and Richard laughed in delight. "Okay, then, how about we just forget about this and go get some ice cream?" She wasn't completely mollified, but ice cream did sound like a wonderful idea.

It was a few days before Richard appeared again at her door. "I need to talk to you, Kiddo," he said as he crossed the threshold. His expression was uncharacteristically serious, and Margie wondered if he was angry with her for the things she had said to him the other day or possibly for some other reason, although she couldn't imagine what she might have done to displease him.

"C'mon in." She motioned toward the living room, closed the door, and followed him to the sofa, frowning in puzzled anticipation.

Richard sat and leaned forward, resting his forearms on his thighs and clasping his hands between his knees, obviously apprehensive about the reason for his visit. Margie sat facing him with one foot curled under her, waiting discontentedly to learn why he had come and what was causing him such consternation. At length he blurted, "What would you say if I told you I've enlisted in the Army."

It took a moment for the words to register, and when they did, Margie was aghast; this was the last thing she had expected. "You've already joined?" she asked incredulously. World War II had been over for almost a year, so it wasn't Richard's safety that concerned her (she had long ago abandoned the idea that a missing limb would be romantic); it was her prospective loneliness once he was gone.

"It's only for eighteen months; it'll give you time to grow up a bit," he teased. "Just don't change too much." He turned and grinned at her. "I kinda like you the way you are."

Margie ducked her head, attempting to hide the smile she couldn't restrain and the blush that was creeping up to her cheeks. After a moment, she again looked at him and asked, "What made you decide to join the Army?" She was struggling with the concept of being unable to see Richard on a fairly regular basis. Her world would be grossly altered without his more or less constant presence and devoted vigilance on her behalf.

Richard shrugged. "I'm not sure yet what I want to do with my life. This will maybe give me the chance to figure some things out. And it's good experience, no matter what I decide to do afterward."

Margie thought her heart would break, and she struggled to keep her tears in check. How could he just go away and leave her? Didn't he realize what that would do to her? "Will you write to me?" she entreated.

He sat up, placing his hands on his knees. "Only if you write me back."

She nodded. "Of course I will. How soon do you leave?"

"In two weeks." Richard sat back against the cushions and folded his arms across his chest. "I was hoping that maybe we could go out to dinner or maybe a show or something before I go. You want to?"

"Sure!" Margie was gratified that he wanted to share some of his last days of freedom with her, and she would happily take as many of them as he was willing to offer.

A few days–to Margie it seemed eons–later, Richard phoned. "Hey, Kiddo, you ready for our date?"

"When?" Margie asked, anxious for the event.

"I've got dinner reservations for Thursday night." he answered. "I can pick you up about seven. Is that okay?"

"I'll have to ask Mom. Just a second." Permission was requested as a formality only; Margie knew there would be no objection but respected her parents' authority. She returned to the phone. "She says I can go."

"Swell. I'll see you Thursday then."

Notwithstanding the fact that Richard, by his own choice, spent an inordinate amount of time in Margie's company, it never crossed her mind that he may be romantically attracted to her, believing as she did that his constant flirtations were merely an attempt to embarrass her–a popular pastime with all of the male gender, as far as she could tell. She was, after all, not quite eleven, but even if she were older, they were too close of kin to allow a seriously amorous relationship. She, therefore, tried to convince herself that her love for Richard, though intense, was nothing more than familial.

Richard, on the other hand, was undisturbed by their close biological kinship. He was, indeed, in love with the unsuspecting child and willing to wait for her. He had given deep consideration to the possibility of producing peculiar children, should they someday marry as he hoped. But there were preventive measures that might be taken to avoid that eventuality; he had never considered himself to be "daddy" material anyway.

Thursday arrived and Margie, at all times striving to please Richard, took special care with her appearance in preparation for their evening together. She had just in the last week begun experimenting on her own with different hairstyles, copying the fashions of some of the older girls at church. She was particularly fond of the look created by brushing her long tresses back to the crown of her head and placing them through a rubber band–a vogue just becoming popular with the teenage crowd and referred to as a "ponytail." When Margie proudly modeled her new "do" for her father's approval, however, George's critical observation was that it "looks just like a horse's tail!" This, of course, delighted Margie. "That's the whole idea, Daddy!" she giggled.

George shook his head in mock dismay. "Folks I know do all in their power to avoid looking like a horse's behind!"

"George!" reprimanded Grace from another room as Margie spurted out a chortle and her father grinned at her conspiratorially. Then he winked.

"Your hair looks fine," he admitted.

Trusting that the style added some maturity to her visual aspect, Margie chose it for her "date" with Richard. She then donned her favorite black skirt and light blue sweater set and glanced hopefully in the mirror. She was not altogether pleased with what she saw. The eyes were too small, the face too round, the hair color too dishwater, and the body a little too–she balked at the word–chubby. Maybe she could swallow a tapeworm; that oughta do the trick–except for her mouse-colored hair. A little makeup might have helped but was out of the question; Grace would never allow it, even for a special occasion. She supposed that this was as good as it was going to get, so she added a splash of perfume behind her ears and on her wrists and waited for her cousin to arrive.

"You look nice tonight," Richard observed as he helped Margie into his mother's car, on loan for the evening. She acknowledged the compliment with a slight smile, pleased that her extra primping had been appreciated. Then, as Richard climbed in behind the wheel, she asked, "Where are we going?"

"It's a surprise. But I think you'll like it," he said.

Though Margie's parents were well-to-do, her family didn't frequent expensive restaurants as a rule, only during those rare times when they accompanied her father to the east coast as he conducted business with the Air Force. When at home, on the few occasions when they did go out, they usually preferred family-type dining rooms. So, when Margie and Richard arrived in Hollywood, she was breathless with excitement.

"I've never been here before," she exclaimed.

"You've never been to Hollywood?" He was doubtful. "How could you live all your life an hour away and never come here?"

"I don't know. Mom and Dad just never brought me."

"Well, well, that makes this all the more fun then. Keep your eyes open; you may see some movie stars, especially once we get to the Brown Derby."

"Is that where we're going?" Margie couldn't disguise her exhilaration, though she would have preferred to act nonchalant and worldly. "Can just anyone go there?"

Richard laughed. "Anyone who calls far enough ahead to get reservations. Actually, I have a friend with connections who was able to wangle it for us."

Richard parked the car, helped Margie alight, and the two of them entered the famous celebrity haunt. Men in suits and women in finery surrounded the tables, each engrossed in their own conversation, with subdued laughter erupting here and there, accompanied by the subtle clanking of dishes and silverware. Richard and Margie were shown to a table, and as they were seated, Margie gazed around the room, straining to see every face, hoping that at least one might be familiar. "I don't see any movie stars," she said, disappointed.

"Well, the night's young. Someone may still show up," Richard assured her as he picked up his menu. "Meanwhile, what do you want to eat?"

Margie examined her choices and finally shrugged. "Why don't you pick something?" she suggested. "Anything's okay except for fish." She wrinkled her nose. "Blagh!"

Richard laughed. "My sentiments exactly! Fish should only be eaten by other fish." He reexamined the menu and eventually ordered roast lamb for both of them. After a bit of a wait–during which Margie, with high expectations, relentlessly watched the flow of newcomers being shown to their tables–the meal was served. It was well prepared and delicious, but Margie had a difficult time concentrating on her food. The atmosphere around them was charged with a certain energy that made it almost impossible for her to sit and calmly eat. She dreamed, as did most girls her age, of someday herself becoming a movie star, although deep down she suspected that it was not a realistic aspiration, just something to fantasize about.

"How's your meal?" asked Richard.

"Oh, it's good," replied Margie, quickly taking a bite of meat. "Do you come here a lot?"

"Oh, no," Richard laughed. "The pocketbook couldn't

handle it too often."

Margie puzzled over that for a moment, a bit concerned about the extravagance. "So why did you bring me here?"

Richard chewed and swallowed before answering. "I wanted to give you something special to remember me by while I'm gone."

Margie's eyes sparkled. "Oh, I'll never forget this." She speared another piece of the lamb and had it halfway to her mouth when a hush fell over the room. Margie looked up to see a striking couple making their way to a reserved table at the back. She watched, awestruck, until they were seated, then leaned toward Richard and asked, "Was that Dana Andrews?"

Richard nodded. "Looked like him."

Margie took a second peek, finding it difficult not to stare. As she turned back, Richard was delighted to note the unconcealed excitement evident in her whole being. She'd actually seen a movie star, and not just any movie star, but Dana Andrews. Just the thought made her heart beat faster. She finished her meal in relative silence, absorbed in the glamour that encircled her.

"Are you about ready to leave?" Richard asked all too soon.

Margie unwillingly nodded. "Okay." She wiped her mouth on her linen napkin, placed it by the side of her plate, took one last sip of water, and rose from her seat. Richard tucked her hand inside his elbow as he led her from the restaurant, but she was almost oblivious to the gallant gesture. She hardly felt her feet touch the ground on the way to the car, and on the ride home, spoke only in monosyllables, her head spinning with the evening's events. She was still young enough to be completely enthralled at the sight of a celebrity and couldn't wait to tell her friends at church all about it.

Then, as Richard walked her to her door, he brought her back down to earth with the comment, "I may not see you again before I leave for boot camp."

Margie nodded in submission as they stepped up onto the porch. "Okay," she said, although it was anything but okay. She wanted to beg him not to go but knew that he was already committed, and that she was powerless to change his chosen course.

Richard observed her forlorn countenance, then turned her toward him and put his arms around her. Margie hugged his waist and leaned her head against his chest. "I'll be home again before you know it," he assured her, resting his chin on the top of her head. "So, be good while I'm gone. Keep me in your happy thoughts, and try not to break too many hearts."

This brought Margie's head up abruptly. "Oh, Richard," she demurred with a sigh, "I'm not the type to break hearts."

"Don't be too sure, Kiddo," he replied. "I'm afraid for my own!" Margie tittered shyly as she broke their embrace. "And don't forget to write."

"I won't," she replied, ducking her head. "I promise."

Richard lifted her chin, gazed at her with a look that Margie could not interpret, then placed a kiss on her forehead. "See ya later," he said.

"Bye, Richard."

He climbed into the car, waited for her to be safely inside the house, then gave her one last wave and pulled out of the driveway.

Chapter VI

Autumn had forever been Margie's favorite season. Most people, she supposed, considered spring to be the time of renewal and rebirth, but she always felt a happy revitalization with the coming of fall. This year carried an additional degree of excitement: Margie had entered the seventh grade in September and was thrilled over the prospect of attending junior high. She had always loved academics and had formerly, because of outstanding scholarship, been advanced one grade. She looked forward to the added challenge. She quickly became engrossed in her studies, endeavoring to maintain a high level of achievement.

Richard was never out of her thoughts, although she had yet to receive a letter and he'd already been gone for seventy-three days. Every afternoon, she had fruitlessly checked the mailbox, but after more than two months with no word, she sadly despaired of any correspondence from her cousin, in spite of his promise. Her normally sunny disposition began to wane. The only thing now that brought her satisfaction was schoolwork, so she redoubled her efforts and surpassed all former accomplishments. Her teachers were gratified, even thrilled. It wasn't often that they had the privilege of tutoring a student so dedicated and single minded. Some of the more sensitive, however, were mildly concerned about her diminished vitality and sudden decline in socialization with her peers.

Fortunately, with the advent of the Christmas holidays, there was a positive change in Margie's demeanor. She couldn't help but catch the festive spirit in the Nelson household, regardless of her troubled heart. It was the one time of year when Grace threw caution to the wind and overrode her natural inclination toward frugality; her children were the imminent beneficiaries.

Every December, Margie and her brother, Jack, made it a point to discover all of their mother's hiding places and, by the time the great day arrived, each knew exactly what "Santa" would bring. There was never a scarcity! Margie seldom received less than everything her heart desired and usually even a little more than she had asked for.

On Christmas Eve, Grace's sisters and their families arrived for the annual dinner at the Nelson home, a lavish occasion joyously anticipated by the adults and children alike. The table talk centered around the family members' activities since they had last been together, with occasional interjections from Jon, whose highly developed sense of humor had recently come to light. He was amazingly perceptive for a fifteen year old and gladly shared his hilarious observations with the gathered family. Margie was enjoying herself tremendously until Aunt Leone diverted the conversation to the one subject that Margie was trying to forget.

"What do you hear from Richard?" she asked her sister.

Aunt Vera looked up from her plate, quickly swallowing a forkful of potatoes. "He seems to be doing all right. I don't think they're feeding him very well, though. He says he's lost some weight. And I know they work him too hard."

"Ahhh, don't worry about him," objected George, sucking his teeth and waving his fork in a gesture of dismissal. "The Army will do him good! Teach him to be a man."

Vera was slightly affronted but kept her own counsel and returned to her meal in silence. People seldom contradicted George; he had a presence that demanded respect and engendered confidence, and in some cases, trepidation. Margie smiled to herself at the exchange. She understood that her father's imperious persona concealed a soft heart but also realized that George's business associates and many of his family and friends were slightly intimidated by him. Nevertheless, Margie believed that he could do no wrong and was secure in the knowledge that her esteem for him was fully reciprocated.

During the discussion of Richard's welfare, Margie's sense of rejection again surfaced. Possibly, once he had left home and begun associating with a worldlier contingent of society, Richard had lost interest in his young cousin. Could he have changed so much in such a short time? She pushed the food around on her plate, no longer hungry, and shut out the lively conversation that surrounded her until the meal was finished, then unobtrusively left the table and headed toward her bedroom.

The three sisters pushed back their chairs and began removing the remains of the meal. "Let me wash the dishes," offered Aunt Vera.

Grace objected. "You don't need to bother; I'll just stick them in the dishwasher."

"It's no bother," contradicted her sister. "Besides, it's the only way I can get my fingernails clean!" This brought a laugh from the other women as they followed each other into the kitchen.

Margie closed the bedroom door behind her and sat on the edge of the bed. The holiday mood of the evening had been destroyed for her as Richard's absence and apparent lack of regard had been brought painfully into focus.

There came a light tap on her door. Margie didn't feel like talking to anyone, but good manners had been ingrained in her too deeply to simply ignore the would be interloper.

"Who is it?" she called, in what she hoped was a normal tone of voice.

"It's Grandma. Do you mind some company?"

Margie was relieved. "Course not, Grandma. C'mon in."

The door opened and the older woman entered and joined Margie on the bed. "Are you okay, Honey?" she asked with a look of concern.

Margie shrugged. "It's just that I haven't heard from Richard, and he promised he'd write. And then, when everyone at the table started talking about him, it reminded me of how much I miss him. But I guess he doesn't miss me at all. In fact, I'm afraid he's forgotten all about me."

Grandma wrapped her arm around Margie's shoulders and pulled her close. "Oh, now, there could be a lot of reasons why he hasn't written. He would never forget you; you're his favorite! Just give him some time to come to grips with his new life. He'll write. Just wait and see." The kind words consoled her; it helped just to have someone tell her that everything would be all right. Margie went to bed that night encouraged by her grandmother's assurances. She would surely hear from Richard soon; if her grandma said so, it must be true. Meanwhile, there was Christmas to think about.

Shortly before dawn, Margie entered her parents' bedroom and crossed to Grace's side of the bed. "Mo-o-om," she sang. "It's time to get u-u-up." Margie had not yet outgrown her excitement over Santa Claus, longing to still believe and, in truth, almost doing so.

Grace moaned softly, rolled over to face Margie, and inquired huskily, "What time is it?"

"Five thirty."

Another moan escaped from Grace as she sluggishly shook George's shoulder. "Wake up, Dear. Our incorrigible daughter wants to open presents."

George's head turned toward his wife's voice as his eyes slowly blinked open. "What time is it?" he reiterated.

"Never mind," Grace mumbled. "You don't want to know." Then, to Margie, "Is Jack awake?"

"Not yet. I'll go get him."

"Okay. Well, go have some toast and orange juice. We'll be right there."

Margie hated her mother's relentless mandate that they have some sort of breakfast before diving into their heavily laden stockings. Nevertheless, she grudgingly obeyed, with Jack joining her in the kitchen.

A few minutes later, they heard their dad's voice bellowing with mock impatience from the living room. "Where are those lazy kids? Aren't they out of bed yet? Let's get this show on the road!" George liked to play the indulgent parent, but was, in fact, pleased at Margie's Christmas morning eagerness. He hoped she would never be too old or too disillusioned to become ardent over anticipated joys.

Another of Grace's immutable rules was that only one present could be opened at a time, so that everyone could see what everyone else received. This was pure agony for her daughter, especially when Grace insisted on painstakingly opening her own gifts in such a way that the wrapping could be preserved for use again another year.

The gift-opening ceremony took most of the morning and, as usual, there were few surprises for Margie under the tree. She almost wished that she hadn't been so conscientious in her prior relentless search of the house. But wait! There was one big surprise. Margie had not received the navy blue skirt that she knew must still be hanging in her mother's closet, completely forgotten (except by Margie). This would require immediate action–crucially subtle–on Margie's part; otherwise it could be months before Grace became aware of her oversight.

Margie followed her mother into the kitchen and watched as Grace made sandwiches from last night's leftover turkey. "Thanks for all the Christmas presents, Mom," she began her campaign. "I especially like the red sweater with the white stripes. It's just what I wanted."

"You're welcome. I'm pleased that you like it."

"I do. I love it! I've been wanting one like that forever!"

"Well, I'm glad you got what you wanted." Grace continued spreading mayonnaise on the slices of bread. This was going to be harder than Margie had thought. She pondered for a moment before an idea struck.

"I think I'll wear it on my first day back at school. Will it look okay with my black skirt?"

Grace turned a puzzled face toward her daughter. "I thought you'd wear it with the navy blue one."

Margie widened her eyes in innocence. "I don't have a navy blue one."

Grace rested her hands on the counter and tilted her head to one side. Then, as realization dawned, she threw up her hands in exasperation. "Oh my goodness!" She hurried to her room and retrieved the coveted garment, as Margie patted herself on the back at her own cleverness.

Chapter VII

It was late in the spring before Margie, at long last, received her first letter from Richard.

Dear Margie,
Sorry it has taken me so long to write. I know I promised and have let you down. But rest assured you have been constantly in my heart and in my thoughts. Not a day has passed but what I've remembered our good times together and longed for the day when they can be continued. Not much chance here to play the piano, nor any fans to listen, even if I did! I miss you, Kiddo!

Margie smiled broadly. This was music to her ears, even without a piano. The letter went on:

I've spent the last few months trying to figure out a few things. Being here has given me lots of time to mull over what I want in life. And I'm thinking the Army might be a good career for me. This hasn't been a lot of fun so far, but if I stay in long enough I could have a pretty good life, I think. Might even get to travel and see the world a bit, like I've always wanted to do. What do you think? We'll see. Haven't really made up my mind yet.

Margie's brow furrowed. The thought of Richard traveling the world while she sat at home was not a happy one. Hopefully, this was just a passing fancy that Richard would soon discard.

The guys here are a pretty rough bunch. But I'll try not to get too corrupted. I still want you to like me when I get home. The routine's grueling and the food's terrible–and that's the easy part. The hard part is that I miss your funny little face. You'd better send me a picture, or better yet, a bunch of pictures. I want to keep track of how pretty you're getting. Remember to be good, Kid, and to keep me in your happy thoughts.

Love always,

Richard

Margie hugged the treasured letter to her chest, tears moistening her cheeks. Richard was still Richard! She immediately sat at her desk and drew out a piece of stationery and a pen.

Dear Richard,

I was so happy to hear from you! I was afraid you had forgotten all about me. Things here are not nearly as exciting as what you're doing. Mainly I just go to school, come home, do homework, eat dinner, and go to bed. I went to the show last night with Mom, Dad, and Jack. We saw "The Best Years of Our Lives" with Dana Andrews! I still can't believe we saw him at the Brown Derby. The show made me cry.

We had a history test at school yesterday. I got 100% (the only one in the class). We're having a ping-pong tournament during lunch time. So far I've beat all my matches, even against the boys. Do you like to play ping-pong? Maybe we can have a game when you get home!

Your mom, Aunt Leone, Uncle Ted, Jon and the twins went with us to the beach last Saturday. Grandma came, too. We took a picnic. It was fun except for the sand in my food. And I got really, really sunburned, so Mom spread Kip all over me that night and wrapped me up in gauze like a mummy. Now I'm getting blisters.

I'm planning a slumber party for Friday night. Mom says that's a funny name for it because no one "slumbers!" Ha! Ha! Hopefully, she'll let me sleep all day Saturday!

Well, guess I'd better go. I've got lots of homework to do.

Love,

Margie

Margie rode high on Richard's letter, pulling it out at every opportunity, reading and rereading the precious words, especially the part about how he missed her. The pages were worn thin by the time his second letter arrived.

Hey Kiddo,

You still my girl? My guess is that the boys there are starting to swarm around. But you can tell them for me that your heart is already spoken for!

Margie smiled at that. Even though she knew that it was all in jest, it still thrilled her to hear Richard talk that way.

I doubt that you'd be interested in what goes on around

here. Just a bunch of guys learning how to fight. A lot of them have girls at home waiting for them. They get pretty lonely. Mail call is a big deal in this neck of the woods. It's the thing that keeps us going. (That's a hint, Kiddo! I know I'm the world's worst at writing, but I still want you to keep those little epistles coming my way.)

We do get to go into town occasionally. Most of the guys like to drink and carouse. Pretty hard sometimes not to join them, but I promised you it would never happen again, remember?

Oh, there is one thing you might like to know. They found out that I can blow a horn, so they've got me playing reveille every morning, a dubious honor since that means I have to be up before everyone else. Oh well, hasn't killed me yet!

Now for the important stuff. I've pretty much decided that Army life is not for me, not on a permanent basis. So I've applied to a couple of music schools. Not sure yet how I'll earn a living when the time comes, but maybe I can turn my meager talents into some kind of career. What do you think?

Take care of yourself and keep me in your happy thoughts.

Love always,

Richard

Margie was ecstatic! Richard would be coming home, at least until he had to leave for college. Again, several weeks passed with no word; then the news she had been waiting for finally arrived.

My Dear Margie,

Well, my stint in the Army is winding down. Won't be long now before I'm back there pestering you again.

Did you get the picture I sent? A real live G.I. Joe,

wouldn't you say?

Margie had not only received the photo, she had never since been parted from it–a handsome Richard in uniform, leaning back against a Jeep, arms folded and legs crossed. She sighed now, just thinking about it.

Can't wait to join you on the piano bench. Have you been practicing? I'm sure we could come up with some jazzy duets! I'll bet I can still beat you at canasta.

Margie was slightly miffed at that. As she recalled, the winnings at the canasta table had been pretty evenly divided.

Well, it's lights out. Be good, and keep me in your happy thoughts.
Love always,
Richard

The rest of the year dragged by and, in the middle of December, Margie received a phone call. "Hey, Kiddo," said a familiar voice. "You want to go looking at cars with me?"

Margie's heart began to pound. "Richard! You're home!"

He chuckled. "Yeah, and I need a car. Want to help me pick one out?"

"Sure!" she laughed. This was so like him, dropping out of the blue and acting like they'd been together just yesterday.

"Good!" he exclaimed. "I'll be by in about thirty minutes, if that's okay with you."

"I'll be ready."

Margie's hands shook as she ran a comb through her hair and put on a little makeup–a little more, actually, than what her mother had agreed was appropriate for a twelve year old, but Grace never seemed to notice (she may have thought that Margie was just growing prettier all on her own, or perhaps Grace was merely choosing her battles).

Soon the doorbell rang and Grace called out, "Richard's here." Margie suddenly couldn't breathe. It had been so long since she'd seen him, she was a little afraid. What if she were a disappointment to him? What if she couldn't think of anything to talk about? What if she acted stupid? What if? What if? What if? What if she just unexpectedly became ill and told him she couldn't go?

Margie took a deep breath, pasted on a pleasant expression, grabbed her wallet, and walked slowly into the living room. "Hi, Richard," she said.

He smiled. "Hey, Kid." He stood with his thumbs hooked in the front pockets of his jeans, looking incredibly attractive and taking in the sight of her as if trying to make up for all the time he had been away. Margie, self-conscious at his scrutiny, lifted her wallet and thumbed through it as if checking to make sure everything was there. "Well," Richard said finally, "I guess we'd better be off." He stepped forward, took hold of her hand, and winked at her. "We've got places to go, people to see, and checks to write!" Margie laughed joyfully. It was so good to have her dear Richard back home again. And, so far, he didn't seem too put off by her.

It was unseasonably warm for this time of year, with not a cloud in the sky and the temperature in the low seventies. As Richard pulled his mother's car out of the driveway and started down the road, with Margie close beside him, she could barely subdue her elation. The weather was gorgeous, Richard was gorgeous, and Margie was . . . well, judging from the smile on Richard's face, at least acceptable. She wanted to laugh out loud, to tell the world how happy she was. She might have, but then she'd have to explain her outburst to Richard, and that was not an option. She could never expose her true feelings to him; never leave herself open to the rejection which was inevitable. But never mind. As long as she was with Richard, she'd seize whatever happiness she could, for however long it lasted. She knew that someday . . . but she wouldn't think about that right now. Right now, she could pretend that the two of them would be together forever.

They must have covered most of the used automobile dealerships in Los Angeles before Richard finally found a car that fit his needs–and his wallet. It was a 1941 Dodge Coupe, painted bright red with a grey interior. Margie thought it was out of this world. After a short test drive, he pulled the car back onto the lot and turned to his young cousin in the seat next to him.

"What do you think?" he asked. "Do you like it?"

"Sure," she said with a wide smile, running her hands over the rough frieze upholstery. "I think it's neat!"

"Well, that's good, because I plan on you spending a lot of time in it."

"Wha'd'ya mean?" she asked, playing the innocent. She thought she knew what he had in mind but needed to be sure.

"I'm going to show you the town, Kiddo."

Margie's eyes danced, and she would have liked to do so herself. She could imagine nothing more exciting than riding anywhere in this car with Richard behind the wheel.

But his well-intended promise was not to be fulfilled. The very next day, Richard received a belated acceptance letter from one of the music schools to which he had applied. He would need to arrive on campus immediately after the holidays and then would be too far away from home to enable a daily or even weekly commute. Margie had mixed emotions: happy that he would be pursuing the vocation which he loved but miserable over the fact of yet another separation.

The holiday celebrations allowed Richard and Margie a small amount of time together, mostly in company with the rest of the family. It was Christmas Eve, following the annual family dinner. The adults were congregating in the living room for their usual after dinner chat, and the four younger male cousins had disappeared inside Jack's bedroom. Richard sidled up to Margie. "Grab a jacket or something and let's go for a walk," he suggested. She nodded and retrieved her coat from the entry closet. They apprised the family of their plans and left through the front door. It was a frosty night for California, even in December, and Richard took Margie's hand as they ascended the slight incline along the street in front of her house.

"You warm enough?" he asked.

"Yeah."

"You happy tonight?"

"Um, so-so."

"Why just so-so?" he prodded.

Margie sighed. "I wish you didn't have to leave again so soon."

"Seems like all I do lately is leave, doesn't it, Kiddo."

"Yeah."

"Well, if it's any comfort, it's probably harder on me than on you."

She glanced at him quizzically. "You're my best friend in the world, Richard. I hate it when you go away. Just thinking about it makes me sad."

"Hmm, that's good news."

Margie was again puzzled. "What? That I'm sad?"

Richard chuckled. “No, that I’m your best friend.”

“You’re different than anyone else I know,” she confessed.

“Now that sounds like the line some of my Army buddies used to use.”

Margie was again baffled by his words. “Wha’d’ya mean?”

“Never mind. Bad joke.” They took several steps in silence before Richard again spoke. “There’s something I want to say to you about my going away.” He paused, searching for the right words. “It’s just that sometimes we have to do things that we don’t really want to do, just because it’s what we need to do. Does that make sense?”

“Sort of. I know you need to go to school. Is that what you mean?”

“Yeah, that and other things. It’s not that I don’t want to stay here with you; it’s just what I have to do right now. I want to be sure you understand that.”

Margie nodded. “I understand.”

“I’m sorry we didn’t get to ‘do the town’ like I promised. And I’m afraid I won’t be able to come around much before I leave for school. I need to spend all of my time getting ready for my classes. It’s been too long since I’ve touched a piece of music, and if I’m not well prepared, they could easily withdraw their acceptance. This chance is really important to me, Margie, and you’re simply too delightful a distraction.”

Margie smiled to herself and wrote those words on her heart.

For New Year’s Eve, Grace decided that, rather than going out with friends, she would invite her sisters’ families over for a night of games and food and the ushering in of 1948. She and Margie worked together all morning, setting up the card tables and stringing crepe paper streamers across the ceiling of the clubhouse, with bunches of mistletoe hung in strategic places–though who among this group would be availing themselves of their purpose Margie couldn't imagine. Nevertheless, Grace was a stickler for protocol, and who ever heard of a New Year's Eve party without mistletoe? Noisemakers and confetti were laid out at each place, along with the asinine paper hats that were a must (according to Grace).

They then prepared ribbon sandwiches and a pineapple icebox dessert, arranged a large vegetable platter, filled several bowls with potato chips, and mixed a sparkling fruit beverage in the cut glass punch bowl. There was barely time to shower and dress before their guests were due to arrive. Margie donned her brown corduroy skirt, a pink cashmere sweater, and her saddle oxfords, pulled her hair up into a ponytail, and splashed cologne in the usual places, then stood in front of the full length mirror and sighed. Why couldn't she have been blessed with flawless skin, an oval face, and a svelte body? She grimaced at her image, crossed her eyes and stuck out her tongue, and was then saved from further loss of composure by the sound of the doorbell.

Ted and Leone, with Jon and the twins, were the first to make their appearance, followed closely by Vera and Richard, who had stopped on the way to pick up Grandma. Coats were deposited in the master bedroom–the Los Angeles area was experiencing an unusually cold winter that year, they'd even had a trace of snow–and everyone made their way across the back patio to the clubhouse. Jack, Jon, and the twins quickly settled around one card table, Grandma and Aunt Vera joined George and Grace at another, and Uncle Ted, Aunt Leone, Richard, and Margie surrounded the third. The idea was that each group would play one hand of Crazy Eights, with the winning couple moving up one table and the losers moving down. Then the procedure would be repeated until one couple had conquered all.

At 11:30 pm, the games were called to a halt–Grace and George were declared the all-time champions–the others had won and lost about equally–and the radio was tuned in to the celebration on Times Square, the broadcast being delayed to coincide with the striking of midnight on the west coast.

After Richard and Margie had filled their paper plates with refreshments, Richard pulled two chairs together into one corner of the room so they could talk.

"Did you help make all this food?" he asked as they sat down and began to eat.

"Um-hm," Margie nodded.

Richard smiled his approval. "So, you're learning how to cook!"

"Well, I don't know if you could call it cooking, since nothing was done on the stove."

"An insignificant distinction," he assured her, "as long as it satisfies the taste buds and fills the stomach–you know that's the way to a man's heart. But then," he winked, "you've already found the way to mine." Margie loved it when Richard spoke of his undying affection, even if he was only teasing, and even though it never failed to make her blush. "So, how's school this year?" he asked with a grin. "Are you still studying hard, or are the boys starting to turn your head?"

Margie grimaced. "The boys at school are just a bunch of babies."

Richard chuckled. "Then I guess I don't have to worry for awhile yet."

George increased the volume of the radio as the announcer indicated the beginning of the final countdown to zero hour; everyone in the room stopped their chatter to chant, "ten . . . nine . . . eight . . . seven . . . six . . . five . . . four . . . three . . .

two . . . one . . .”

Richard glanced toward the ceiling, beckoning with his head for Margie to follow his gaze. There, a few feet above them, she beheld a sprig of mistletoe. As Margie lowered her chin, Richard leaned over and kissed her gently on the lips, sending her heart into serious arrhythmia. She pulled back and searched his face for some sign of playfulness, bewildered by the apparent sincerity of his gesture, and found no evidence there that he had been merely baiting her. She lowered her eyes, blushing. “Happy New Year, Kiddo,” Richard whispered. She looked up into his eyes, seeking the twinkle that would tell her that it had been a joke, just more of his constant teasing, but found instead an expression that she couldn’t read. Then Richard looked away as George demanded everyone’s attention by clanging a spoon against the punch bowl and raising his glass as he offered a toast to “many more new years together as a family.”

“Hear, hear!” was the unanimous response.

The perplexing moment had passed, but the memory of her first real kiss would keep Margie awake that night into the wee hours, puzzling over its meaning. She couldn’t conceptualize the idea that Richard might love her the way that she loved him. She lay pondering the inherent complications associated with a serious relationship between first cousins. Tossing about from side to side, she tried to turn her mind off, to smother thoughts of Richard, to be rational rather than hopeful–there was no future in hopeful. The last time she looked at the clock, it read 3:00 am.

At 3:00 am, Richard was also wide awake. What had he done? He had lost control, had let a fleeting impulse ruin everything. He had always purposely kept his mood light around Margie, not wanting to divulge his true feelings until she was old enough to understand. And now he had blown it! He'd seen the look in her eyes after that unplanned, unforgivable, unbelievably sweet kiss: something between surprise and panic. Would she ever again look at him with that trusting expression that he adored? He wanted to kick himself for being such an idiot.

Richard left town two days later without seeing Margie again. She was both disappointed and relieved. It would be embarrassing to face him right now, wondering if she had read more into that kiss than he had intended. Better to put a little time and space between them for awhile. Perhaps Richard felt the same way, thinking the kiss was a mistake.

There were no letters this time–probably best, thought Margie, under the circumstances. Maybe the silence would allow them to forget about New Year's Eve, pretend it never happened, and simply resume their old camaraderie.

Finally, toward the end of his first semester of study, Richard telephoned. "How's my girl?" he asked.

"I'm fine," she assured him, relieved that his voice indicated no sign of discomfort.

"Sorry I haven't been in touch."

"That's okay. I know you've been busy. How soon are you coming home?"

"In a couple of weeks. Then maybe we can hit the beach together." This was the old Richard talking, and Margie's troubled mind was inexpressibly eased.

"That'd be fun!" she said. "I love going to the beach!"

"Yeah," he chuckled, "I know."

Richard was obliged to obtain summer employment immediately upon his return, but he and Margie spent most of their Saturdays at the ocean, picnicking and riding the waves, intermittently collapsing on their beach towels and talking with the old easiness as they lay side by side, eyes closed against the glaring sun.

"So, what do you plan to be when you grow up?" Richard asked, teasing. He knew that, at thirteen, Margie already considered herself something of an adult. And, in truth, she was mature beyond her years.

"What do you mean when I 'grow up'?" she chided.

He laughed and turned on his side toward her, resting his head on one hand. "Okay, then, when you graduate from high school, or college, if that's where you're headed."

"Yeah, that's where I'm headed. But I don't know what I want to do yet." Margie squinted into the sun. "I've thought about being a school teacher, but they usually turn out to be old maids."

"Well, if you end up an old maid and I end up an old bachelor, we can always get married and save the family honor," he suggested, grinning at her.

Margie laughed and playfully backhanded him on the shoulder. "But I don't want to end up an old maid," she said. "I want to have twelve kids."

"Twelve!" Richard almost shouted. "Heaven help us! Why so many?"

"I don't know. It just seems like it would be fun to have a big family."

"Well, yeah, but there's big, and then there's BIG!" he said. "Do you really think it's feasible to try to raise a family that size in this day and age? Things are different now than they were in Grandma's time, you know."

"I know. I guess I'll just have to marry someone rich."

Richard's eyes clouded, the merriment suddenly gone. "Would that make you happy? A rich husband?"

Margie was puzzled by his unexpected gravity. "Well," she

equivocated. "I would have to be in love, of course. But I wouldn't complain if he happened to own a few oil wells."

Richard pulled himself to a sitting position, rested his forearms on his bent knees, and looked toward the ocean. He and Margie had never before discussed her desire for children, and her revelation troubled him. Though he hadn't yet seriously broached the subject of marriage with Margie, he had, in his own mind, always assumed that they could be happy together with no one but themselves. He also suspected that he would never be rich. "Well, it's not only the money," he continued, pleading his case. "This world is a tough place to raise kids."

Margie sensed some vexation in his tone and sat up, curling her legs to one side and studying his profile. "Yeah, I guess." She was uncomfortable with his altered demeanor, and turned the conversation slightly. "Do you ever wish that you had brothers and sisters?"

"Nah, I like things the way they are, nice and quiet."

Margie had always been curious about Richard's early home life–she couldn't imagine a family with no siblings and only one parent–but had never before found a timely way to bring it up.

"Was it difficult for you when your mom left your dad? I mean, were you close to him? Have you ever resented her for it?"

"It's pretty hard to feel close to someone who beats you," he acknowledged.

"Your dad beat you?" Margie was astonished. She had never before heard a disparaging comment about his father, from his mom or anyone else in the family. "Is that why your mom left?"

Richard shrugged. "I dunno. Part of it maybe. The main

reason, I think, is because he started drinking and then couldn't hold down a job; kinda turned into the town bum. You know, the usual scenario."

"Did he ever hurt your mom? When he was drunk, I mean."

"Depends on what you mean by 'hurt.' I never noticed anything, but I was just a kid. The bruises he gave her weren't on the outside where I could see them."

Margie perceived Richard's anger even though he still was not looking at her, but she couldn't let the subject drop. She was intrigued by the enigma of a sensitive, caring individual like Richard coming from such an abusive environment. "So, what happened to your dad? Where is he now?"

"Drunk himself to death. At least that's the way I see it. Drove his car into a tree one night, about five years ago, when he was so soused up he couldn't see straight."

"I'm sorry. Not for him, for you."

Richard shrugged. "Things are what they are. No use worrying about what can't be changed." He rocked up on his feet, stood and reached down a hand to Margie. "How about a swim? I'll race you to the water."

Margie grabbed his hand, jumped up, and ran full speed to the ocean's edge, but could in no way out-sprint her cousin. She was a good, strong swimmer, however, and lagged only slightly behind as they rode several waves into shore. Finally, exhausted, they fell, laughing, onto their towels.

"How did you learn to swim so well?" Richard asked.

"Jack and I have races all the time."

"Who wins?"

She grinned at him. "It's usually a tie," she said, her eyes sparkling.

Chapter VIII

That fall, Margie entered high school, and Richard, once again, left town. Letters were exchanged infrequently as they both became absorbed in their separate involvements. There were dances at church, where Margie constantly met new boys, and was soon dating one or another of them on an occasional basis. Richard was meanwhile doing his share of entertaining the young women he met at the conservatory.

In addition to her studies, Margie indulged her love of sports by joining a school-sponsored association, which met after hours and involved extracurricular athletic events. She was thus afforded the opportunity to make many new friends, and she soon found herself deluged with invitations to join some of the more elite campus clubs, organized and peopled by the "popular" contingent at school. This left her slightly bedazzled; she had never considered herself to be of their ilk. Though she accepted membership in a few such groups, she felt slightly ill at ease at their meetings. There didn't seem much point to them, other than gossip and refreshments–and she could do without both. Still, it kept her occupied and added some variation to her days.

The coming summer didn't afford Richard the lazy Saturdays of the year before. He was putting in extra hours at work and holding down a second job as well in an effort to better secure his future self-reliance. His nights were usually free, but Margie's were not. She was participating on her church softball and volleyball teams, had been cast in a three-act play with rehearsals twice a week and, in addition, was spending many of her evenings with church friends, planning and executing beach parties, an activity which, like her club meetings, consisted exclusively of gossip and food, but of which, in this case, Margie totally approved (they were, after all, held at the beach).

Richard still stopped by occasionally, and Margie was always delighted to see him, but as she became more and more preoccupied with her own personal pursuits, she became less and less available to Richard. This was the expected scenario that he had always anticipated with apprehension. She was, he realized, something of a free spirit, and it was inevitable that the time would come when she must spread her wings and explore all of life's possibilities. He could only hope that at the end of her flight, however long the journey, she would eventually return to perch at his side.

As for Margie, though her love for Richard never diminished–he was always there in some part of her mind–she knew that she must broaden her scope. She wasn't sure how she would do it but understood that she must. It was time to start thinking about her future, and for obvious reasons, it was pointless to consider Richard an integral part of her plans.

The end of summer was rapidly and regrettably approaching, and a group of Margie's school friends were, as a result, planning a "Back to School Bash." It would be held at the posh home of one of the more–how to describe her?–sophisticated girls, one with whom Margie was not well acquainted. Still, there would be a few of her closer friends in attendance, so she anticipated an enjoyable evening.

Her brother had been coerced into dropping her off at the party, since he was going out anyway. He had agreed, with the stipulation that she be willing to arrive an hour late so that he wouldn't have to return home before his date. Jack deposited her at the curb and then executed a speedy getaway before she had even rung the doorbell. The front door was jerked open by a young man whom Margie had never before met, and from behind him, the cacophony of young revelers assaulted her ears. She stepped over the threshold and was immediately taken aback by the sight before her. While many of the male attendees were engaged in their usual horsing around for the benefit of the giggling girls, several couples were standing or sitting along the perimeter of the living room, wrapped in each other's arms, openly necking. The furniture had been moved back, and a few were dancing–she guessed that's what they called it. There wasn't much discernable footwork, and it was difficult to ascertain where one partner's outline ended and the other's began.

Margie was intensely tense. She searched desperately for a friend, but it appeared that those she had counted on had not shown up. She had no choice but to stay; her parents were at the movies and wouldn't be available to pick her up for a couple of hours. She would simply attempt to remain invisible. Maybe she could hide out in the dining room and pretend that she was serving at the refreshment table.

She made her way unobtrusively through the crowd and seated herself around the corner next to the punch bowl. At least here she wouldn't have to observe the offensive behavior in the other room. She picked up a cookie and began nibbling, wondering how she could possibly entertain herself for two more hours. She could, of course, eat cookies the whole time, or at least as long as they lasted. Not a bad idea, if it weren't for the unsightly consequences.

At that moment, a young man she recognized from one of her classes the year before–was his name Ken?–turned the corner of the dining room, evidently to sample the refreshments, and noticed Margie sitting there alone. He did a double take and then asked, "You wanna dance?"

He seemed a little less boisterous than the boys who were making so much ruckus in the other room, so Margie decided to take a chance. Ken took her hand and led her back amidst the zombie-like figures who were still occupying the same positions as when she had, moments before, made her escape. Pulling her into dance posture he observed, "You're Margie, right?" She smiled and nodded. "Yeah," he continued, "I remember you from English class. My third time around; I'm one of those, you know, 'dumb jocks.' Flunked it the first two times. So, how did you like Miss Peters? I thought she was pretty tough on us. Too much homework!"

"Really? I liked her. But then, I like English, so the homework didn't bother me."

"Yeah, if I remember right, you were one of the brains in the class."

Margie blushed. "I just like school, that's all."

"Maybe you could tutor me this year," he suggested with a smile. He was joking, but Margie didn't catch on.

"You'll be a senior. I won't know any of the stuff you're studying."

Ken looked at her like she wasn't quite savvy and changed the subject. "It's hot in here. You want some punch?" Margie agreed, and they made their way back to the dining room, where Ken filled a cup for each of them.

Margie took a sip and frowned. "This tastes kind of funny."

"Seems okay to me," he shrugged. "You want to get some air?" He didn't wait for an answer but took her by the elbow and guided her out through the French doors. The patio was unoccupied and the cool breeze was welcome, carrying with it the scent of night blooming jasmine.

Ken motioned her to a love seat and sat down next to her, his arm resting on the back of the seat. "So, are you having a good time?" he asked.

Margie didn't want to hurt his feelings by admitting her all around disappointment and discomfort, so she offered a small fib. "Sure, it's okay."

"Just okay?" He scooted closer still. "Maybe I can do something about that." He leaned over and nuzzled her cheek, then whispered in her ear, "You come with anyone?"

The love seat didn't offer much room to spare, but Margie slid as far away as possible. "No, my brother dropped me off." She was beginning to panic, wondering how she could gracefully disengage herself from a situation that was becoming increasingly galling. "Shall we go back inside? I've cooled off now."

Ken grinned. "I haven't! In fact, I'm getting warmer all the time." With that, he forcibly pulled Margie close and kissed her passionately. Margie shoved her hands against his chest and pushed with all her might, trying desperately to pull away, but he was not only a dumb jock, he was a strong one as well. When he finally came up for air, she squirmed out of his grasp and ran, weeping, into the house.

She quickly located a telephone and dialed Richard's number. When he answered, she began sobbing in relief, "Richard, can you come and get me?"

Richard was immediately alarmed. "Where are you? Are you okay? That was stupid; you're obviously not okay. What happened?"

"I'm at a party and one of the guys gave me some punch and I think it was spiked and then he tried to get fresh with me and . . . please hurry!"

"Tell me where you are."

Margie stuttered out the address and hung up the phone. She then turned and saw Ken leaning against the wall, a smirk on his face. Afraid that he might corner her again, she crossed to the other side of the room and found a chair that was only wide enough for one person. Ten minutes later, the front door burst open as if hit by a battering ram, and Richard's image filled the doorway, his countenance that of an avenging angel. The shocked partiers were stilled by the outrageous intrusion and all eyes were focused, in thrilled anticipation, on the uninvited guest.

Richard surveyed the room until he spotted Margie, who had stood from her chair but was then frozen with apprehension. What kind of showdown had she instigated? She'd never before seen her cousin like this; his anger was palpable. Richard's long strides brought him to her side. "Which one was it?" he demanded.

"It doesn't matter," Margie muttered in an effort to tranquilize the situation. "Let's just go."

But Richard was not to be put off. "Which one?"

Margie slowly lifted a pointing finger, and Richard closed the distance between himself and Ken. Ken backed away as his hands came up, palms forward. "Hey, Fella, no harm … " His last word was lost against Richard's fist as it smashed into his face, loosening a few teeth in the process and knocking Ken firmly to the floor. Ken raised up on one elbow and brushed the back of his hand across his mouth and nose, smearing it with blood and convincing him that he was better off staying put rather than planning any kind of retaliation.

Without a word, Richard grabbed Margie by the arm and fairly lifted her off her feet as he flew out the door to his waiting car. There he stopped and grasped both of her arms just above the elbows, forcing her to face him. "What in the name of heaven were you doing at this kind of party?"

Margie began simpering. "I'm sorry. I didn't know it was going to be like this."

"Use your head, Margie. You could see what was going on when you got here. Why didn't you call me then?"

She was shamefaced. "I don't know. I thought I would be all right until Mom and Dad could come to get me."

Richard shook his head in frustration. "Get into the car," he ordered, for once not even bothering to assist her. Marching around to the driver's side, he practically pulled the door off its hinges getting it open. He fired up the engine with a vengeance and pulled from the curb.

Margie was contrite on the way home, while Richard continued to fume. Finally, when he seemed to have regained control, she offered a meek, "Thank you, Richard."

He glanced over at her and once again shook his head. "You're welcome," he said. He pulled his right hand from the steering wheel and flexed the fingers. "But it'll take awhile for my hand to forgive you."

Chapter IX

Jack had been accepted at the University of Utah, and at the end of August, Margie willingly stayed a few days with her friend Donna's family while Grace and George delivered her brother, along with the entire contents of his cluttered bedroom, to his new living quarters in Salt Lake City. It was anyone's guess where he would put all of his paraphernalia when he got there.

In September, Margie was back to her own educational pursuits, and she was feeling especially important this year, not only because she was now, in effect, an only child, but because she was a mighty sophomore as well. Her fellow students were uncommonly friendly–they were better acquainted than before–and she was often invited, because of her singing and dancing abilities, to participate in special assemblies and other activities. She was also a member of the sophomore class cabinet, a section of the student government, which was involved, along with the faculty, in making decisions that affected her classmates and herself. All in all, it was a busy semester for her, and before she knew it, the Christmas holidays were at hand.

Richard was doing some private tutoring at the conservatory and was not expected home for Christmas or any time before the end of the academic year. Though Margie was disappointed, she was becoming accustomed to his long absences and kept telling herself that it was all for the best anyway.

The semiformal New Year's Eve dance at the church was pretty much a family affair. Many young people dated but just as many went by themselves or with their parents. Since Margie had not been asked by any of the boys, she would be forced to attend in company with George and Grace–a great blow to her ego but not so great that she would consider missing the dance. There was always the hope that she wouldn't spend the whole evening holding up the wall.

Jack, who had flown home for winter break, would also be going stag but probably wouldn't remain that way for long. Considering his blonde good looks, as well as his proficiency on the dance floor, there was a very good chance that he might meet someone interesting and drive her home afterward. He had made arrangements with Grace to borrow her car for the evening, just in case.

Margie had spent the last week at the sewing machine creating something frothy for the occasion and was pleased with the result. The crisscross bodice was fashioned of silver lamé with an empire waist and fitted midriff; the full skirt of pink taffeta, overlaid with several yards of gathered tulle, reached to her ankles. Her accessories included silver high-heels and rhinestone necklace and earrings–she felt virtually elegant.

The evening was cool, but Margie abhorred the idea of a heavy wrap which would, without question, diminish the effect of her grand entrance at the evening's soiree. So when Grace suggested she wear a coat, Margie insisted that she was "already about to die from the heat," which was met with a rolling of the eyes and a shake of the head. Grace was not the least bit fooled; she knew exactly why Margie didn't want to wear a wrap (she had, after all, been young once herself).

Even lacking an escort, Margie's spirits were high as she and her family arrived at the dance. Once inside, she quickly separated herself from her parents and looked for some of her girlfriends who had promised to be there. Spotting Donna and Emily, also sans squires, at the refreshment table, she quickly joined their company.

"Any cute boys?" she asked, discretely scanning the perimeter of the room (as best she could between the couples on the dance floor). "That is, cute boys who aren't attached to girls–cute or otherwise?"

Donna snorted. "Barf, retch! Much as I hate being a wallflower, tonight it beats the alternative. At least the refreshments are good." Suiting action to word, she retrieved two more chocolate chip cookies from the table behind her.

The three girls nonchalantly surveyed the unaccompanied members of the opposite sex who were clustered together across the hall and discussed the virtues and imperfections of each. "That one has possibilities," suggested Emily, indicating a tall, well-groomed boy who was, at that moment, glancing in their direction.

"Too skinny," objected Donna. "What about the guy standing next to him? Didn't notice him before."

"On his right or left?" asked Margie, leaning one way and then the other to see between the members of the crowd.

"I don't know. That direction." Donna motioned to the left with her thumb. "You know I can't remember which is left or right. It helped when I broke my elbow 'cause I knew it was the left one that was crooked. But when I broke the other one, it put me right back where I started." They'd heard the story before, but it never failed to bring a chuckle.

"Oh, oh," she warned. "Don't look now, but I think the drip of our dreams is zeroing in on one of us. I believe I need to go to the restroom right about now!" She dropped her empty paper cup in the waste container and beat a hasty retreat.

"Me, too," announced Emily as she turned on her heel and hurried away behind her friend.

Margie felt sorry for the short, spectacled boy who was quickly approaching and, much as she dreaded the humiliation of actually dancing with him, didn't want to hurt his feelings by following her ill-mannered comrades. Whether by default or premeditation, she didn't know, but she was the one he haltingly invited to dance. Knowing that it would be unforgivably rude to refuse, she smiled and nodded her head.

Fortunately, it was a fast number so they, at least, didn't have to make bodily contact, and any attempt at conversation was, thankfully, an impossibility. But, as the music ended, he kept hold of her hand and remained in the middle of the floor, obviously with no intention of relinquishing his advantage. The band began to play one of Margie's favorite love songs. She rolled her eyes as she caught a glimpse of Donna and Emily standing against the wall, stifling laughter and hiding their grinning faces behind spread fingers. She then turned to her partner, smiled, and allowed him to press her right hand into one sweaty palm, while he placed his other at her waist.

The lights were dimmed to make the most of the mirrored ball suspended from the center of the ceiling, swirling hypnotic flecks of luminance on the walls and floor, and the music was so delicious it brought a lump to Margie's throat. A very romantic setting, if you happened to be with the right person.

"So, what grade are you in?" her clumsy partner finally articulated, struggling to make conversation.

"Tenth. How about you?"

"I'm just a freshman." There was another lengthy interim as they both searched for words to fill the void.

After several torturous minutes, Margie asked, "What school do you go to?"

"Redondo Beach."

"Hmm."

The music came to a stop then, and Margie sighed with relief. But her relentless wannabe suitor maintained his tight grip on her hand until the next dance began, and he pulled her once again into his arms.

"What about you?" he inquired.

"Hmm?" Had Margie missed something?

"What school do you go to?"

"Oh! Westchester."

"Hmm," he nodded. Margie observed that her two friends continued to enjoy her extreme discomfort, and she was beginning to despair of ever escaping this tenacious young Romeo when a hand suddenly came out of nowhere and tapped her little companion on the shoulder.

"May I cut in?" her rescuer inquired, although that particular question was always a mere matter of courtesy; the request was always granted, however begrudgingly.

The boy looked confused–perhaps he'd never been cut in on before; most likely he'd never danced before–and muttered, "Oh. Okay," and, turning, walked away without so much as a "thank you" to his very relieved partner. Margie had by now, of course, identified this knight in shining armor.

"Richard," she gratefully sighed, as he placed his hand at her waist and led her back into the dance. He looked especially debonair this evening, characteristically forsaking the traditional suit and tie worn by every other male in attendance and sporting an open collar under a casual blazer. Margie loved the confident way in which he could invariably snub convention and yet never be out of place. She was so happy to see him that she wanted to cry.

"What on earth are you doing here?" she asked, the lights in her eyes competing with the glitter of the mirrored ball. "I thought you had to stay at school."

"We finished early and I decided I needed to come home and check on my favorite girl," he responded.

She laughed. "But how did you know where to find me?"

"Oh, I have my spies!" he joked. "Actually, your mom told my mom where you were going." He twirled her out under his arm and assessed her appearance as he pulled her back to him, nodding his approval. "I'd say it's a good thing I showed up when I did. The way you look tonight . . ." He shook his head, leaving the sentence unfinished.

Margie colored with pleasure. "So, when did you get home? How long are you here for?"

Richard chuckled. "So many questions," he said. "Why don't you just put your head on my shoulder for now and we'll talk later?"

Margie did as requested, and Richard drew her close, leaning his cheek against her hair and humming along with the band. Margie floated ecstatically through the rest of that number and the next. Then the band played a Glenn Miller favorite, which called for some trickier footwork–no problem for either of them. They loved to jitterbug, and Margie was soon laughing in delight at some of the innovative maneuvers that Richard was executing with great finesse.

The band once again shifted gears, choosing an old favorite, one that held special significance for Margie. As the familiar strains unfolded, Richard leaned his head close and began to sing softly in her ear:

> *I'll be loving you*
> *Always,*
> *With a love that's true*
> *Always.*

The band played on, but Richard stopped singing long enough to remark in his normal blithe way, "You told me once that you would. Remember?"

"Yes," she laughed softly, retrieving the fond memory, "but I'm surprised that you do."

"Oh, I'm not likely to forget that; I plan to hold you to it!"

Margie tilted her head sideways and looked at him with questioning eyes, never altogether sure how much of his folderol she should believe. Gaining no enlightenment from his inscrutable expression, she returned her head to his shoulder and listened as he delivered the remainder of the lyrics. Finally he suggested, "Let's go tell your mom that I'll take you home, and then we'll go for a ride."

"Okay," she agreed.

They walked hand in hand in search of her parents and found them sitting with several of their cronies in a small circle of chairs, enjoying some punch and cookies. Margie interrupted their lively conversation and asked permission to leave with Richard.

"Just don't be out too late," cautioned Grace.

"Well, it is New Year's Eve," Richard pleaded, flashing his irresistible smile at his aunt.

"Yes," Grace retorted, immune to his charm. "And she is only fourteen! And we do have church in the morning."

"Okay," he acquiesced. "We won't be too late." Grace,

smiling, shook her head in surrender and waved them off.

They hurried to the parking lot and climbed into Richard's car, the same car that Margie had helped him pick out–was it only two years ago? As he pulled out onto the street, Richard said, "Now, to answer all your questions. I just got home tonight, and I'll be here for two days. So, I don't have much time. But we do have tonight. Where should we head?"

With only a moment's hesitation, she suggested, "Why don't we drive to the beach?"

"The beach it is," he replied, turning the car in the proper direction. "So, what have you been doing with yourself these last few months? Do you have a boyfriend yet?"

"Sort of," she reluctantly admitted. "There's a boy at school that I've gone out with a couple of times."

"So, where is he tonight?

"His family went to Big Bear to ski this weekend."

"Good riddance!" he joked. Then, in a more serious tone, "Does he treat you okay?"

"Mmm, not as well as you," she said with a smile, "but he's okay. I like him. She pursed her lips and glanced sideways at Richard. "He tells me I'm 'jail bait.' What does that mean?"

Richard groaned. "I worry about you, Kiddo. You're way too naive for your own good. But, as you know by now, if a guy ever gets out of hand in any way, you just say the word and I'll . . . well, you know what I'll do!" He cocked an eyebrow at her and she grinned. She did know, and she loved the way he always made her feel pampered and protected and cherished–not easy for someone as headstrong as she.

"Can we walk on the beach for awhile?" she asked as Richard brought the car to a halt at the side of the road a short distance from the ocean.

"It's a little cool."

"That's okay."

"All right then," Richard answered, setting the brake and turning off the ignition. "Just let me get your door."

Margie always felt stupid when any other boy insisted on opening her door. It's not like both of her arms were broken. But, with Richard, it just seemed right for him to take care of all of the little inconveniences. Perhaps it was because he never did anything just to make an impression–he didn't play the gentleman when it suited his purposes and then abandon the façade when it became unnecessary or inconvenient. He took care of Margie because he genuinely wanted to, because he felt the need to, no matter what the circumstances.

They slipped off their shoes and left them in the car while they scuffed slowly through the soft sand, making their way toward the large rocks that jutted out into the water. It was an unusually clear night, the bright moonlight sparkling on the breakers that pounded noisily onto the wet shoreline. Richard held Margie's hand as they walked and talked, laughing and taunting, savoring the brisk night air. With his prompting, she told him about her involvement in school sports, her love for her creative writing class, and of the trio she had recently joined. "What part do you sing?" Richard asked.

"Alto."

"Why?"

"What do you mean, 'why?'" she asked, puzzled.

"Why are you singing alto when you're a soprano?"

Margie shrugged. "I've always sung alto, ever since I got out of grammar school. In every group I've ever sung with, that's always the part they need. Besides, it's boring to sing melody."

"Oh, I see, you like a challenge!"

"Well, I for sure don't like being bored."

"Hmm. Are you thinking of a career in music?" he asked.

"It's the thing I love most in the world," she said, "but I don't think I'm good enough to be a professional singer."

"Well," he drew the word out, "it's hard to tell until you start training in the proper range. Have you thought about private lessons?"

"Not really. Mom doesn't seem to think I have any future with my voice."

"Yeah, well, maybe mother doesn't always know best. You need to decide what you want."

They walked for awhile in comfortable silence, each with their own thoughts. "Lots of stars tonight," Richard noted.

Margie looked skyward. "Remember when you used to point out all the constellations to me? I still can't find anything by myself except for the dippers, and sometimes I don't even do so well with those." She shivered slightly and rubbed her free hand briskly up and down her other arm.

"You're cold," noted Richard. "Here." He took off his jacket and laid it over her shoulders.

"But now you'll be cold," she said, pulling the lapels together in front of her.

"No, I'm fine," he said. "I've got my love to keep me warm."

"Oh?" Margie stopped, playing along with his nonsense. "Anybody I know?"

Richard turned to face her and shook his head, his jovial demeanor slipping away. "Kiddo, if you haven't guessed by now. . ."

Margie stood still and folded her arms, searching Richard's face intently, at a loss for words. Had he been serious all of these years with all his intimations of love? Surely he understood that there was no possibility for them to become romantically involved. They had no choice but to settle for the status quo: more than friends, less than lovers. Richard was the kindest, smartest, most charming person she knew, and there was nothing she wanted more than to spend the rest of her life with him, but there was no way that they could ever be together–not in the manner at which he kept hinting. Knowing that this was a fact of their lives, Margie had thus far ignored her own desires, but at this moment, she was overwhelmed with frustration. If Richard was really sincere, and Margie was beginning to believe that he might be, then it would be up to her to become the voice of reason. She was positive that her cousin would never assume that role.

"Richard." She pulled her bottom lip between her teeth and looked past his shoulder toward the ocean, tears welling up and beginning to spill. Richard stepped forward and wiped them away with his thumb, forcing her to meet his gaze. "Richard," she repeated, forcing herself to say the words that would break their hearts, "you know there can never be anything romantic between us."

He smiled apologetically. "Too late, Kid."

Margie sighed, not knowing how to respond. "I guess we should be heading home; it's getting late," she said finally, not really wanting to end their time together, but suddenly saddened by the futility of it all.

Later, Richard fretted over the way the evening had turned out. He hadn't intended to expose his true feelings as yet, realizing that it would distress Margie. At this juncture, she was too entrenched in societal norms to even consider something so bizarre as marrying her first cousin. It would take time for her to reach the point where she could simply snub tradition and follow her own instincts, and maybe she never would.

He knew all this and yet had allowed the irrevocable words to fall from his lips, probably setting his campaign back a few years. There was no excuse for his lack of self-discipline, other than it was becoming impossible to continue squelching his overwhelming inclination to tell the world how he felt about his cousin.

There was only one solution: he would have to stay away for awhile, to give Margie some space, allow her the chance to assimilate the episode at the beach. Otherwise, he knew there would be no hope.

Chapter X

By the time Margie was nearing the end of her junior year in high school, Richard was finishing up his music studies. He had added a summer semester to the previous year, not only to accelerate the completion of his degree, but to accomplish a contrived distancing from Margie. They had not seen each other since that night on the beach; he had forced himself to remain at the conservatory, using the time to study and/or teach for the past sixteen months, hoping that it had been time enough for his cousin to regain her composure.

Margie, meanwhile, was bewildered. After their emotional last meeting, it seemed Richard's ardor had quickly chilled. She hadn't heard from him since he returned to school almost a year and a half ago. She knew she had to let him go eventually but not just yet.

One afternoon in May, Margie lay on her bed, contemplating the sudden lapse in Richard's attentions and concluding that he had probably found a serious girlfriend at the conservatory. That eventuality should make her happy; it was stupid and selfish for her to want to claim him as her exclusive property. Their lives were bound to take different directions. It wasn't realistic to expect that they could forever maintain their attachment of past years. Maybe it was time to let go, after all, banish Richard irretrievably from her heart and mind. Would it be possible for her to do that? Could she ever be happy with Richard entirely omitted from her life? She felt a lump in her throat. Perhaps the inevitable separation was already an unwelcome fact.

She was startled out of her reverie as the newly acquired telephone on her nightstand–a birthday gift from her parents–rang. After Margie's "hello," a long-absent voice asked, "How's my girl?"

Margie took a long breath while she gathered her courage. "I don't know, Richard. How is she?"

There was a long pause. "What's that all about?" he finally asked, confused by her response.

"Oh, nothing. You haven't called for awhile."

"Sorry, Kid. Things have been crazy this year," he waffled. "But I'll be home soon and then we can make up for lost time."

"Actually, that's just what I was thinking about." Margie tried to keep her tone aloof. "I believe it might be better for both of us if we only see each other, from now on, at family parties, when it's unavoidable."

There was another lapse as Richard contemplated Margie's detectable antipathy (perhaps justified). "Are you okay, Kiddo?"

Margie sighed. "I'm fine," she said with marked agitation. "I just don't know how to feel about you." Her tone softened. "You've always been the most important person in my life, but you really need to forget about me and find someone you can marry." Margie nearly choked on the word. "Or maybe you have already; I don't know. But, regardless, I need to let go." She began to sob. "I don't know how to do that, Richard." She grabbed a tissue, blew her nose, and ineffectually wiped at her eyes. "How do I do that?"

"You don't."

"I have to!"

"Why? Who's asking you to?"

"You should be."

"But I'm not. And I never will."

"Richard, this whole thing is impossible."

"Listen to me, Margie. If and when you no longer want me around, that'll be the time to let go. Understood?"

Margie sobbed, feeling a guilty kind of relief. "Understood," she said.

"Good. Now, no more silly proclamations. I've got finals coming up and don't have time to worry about what your fertile little mind might be conjuring up."

Margie dreamed that night that she and Richard were planning to sail together to a far away island where they could live forever, joyously, without regard for social mores. Their family was pleased with their decision and understood that this was the only way that either of them could ever be happy.

Margie began to pack her clothes and personal belongings, but forgotten possessions kept falling out of her closet and she felt compelled to leave nothing behind. Frantically she stuffed endless pieces of luggage, but the pile kept growing.

Grace was then standing in her doorway, wearing a sorrowful expression. "Richard can't wait any longer," she said. "The boat is leaving."

"No!" screamed Margie. Suddenly, all of the things that were so important a minute ago became meaningless. She left the bags and ran all the way to the pier where the boat had been docked. There was Richard, a hundred feet off shore, standing on the deck and waving as he moved seaward. "Richard! Come back! Don't leave me here!" But the boat kept moving, and Richard kept waving.

In June, Richard returned home, once again at loose ends about his future. All he wanted was to devote his life to music, but he knew he couldn't make an adequate living teaching piano lessons and wasn't inclined toward working in the school system.

The life of a professional musician had no appeal: playing in a band, constantly on the road traveling from town to town, struggling to survive. No, his musician's heart would have to be content with avocational endeavors. He needed a full time occupation that would "bring home the bacon."

He picked up the phone to call Margie, anxious to see her again and hoping the feeling would be reciprocated. She picked up after the second ring and immediately recognized the caller. From the sound of her voice, Richard concluded that their relationship–whatever it might be (he'd never found a word to adequately describe it)–was still alive and well. They talked for awhile of all the things that had transpired with each of them since they had last spent time together and then made plans for the following night.

Margie informed her parents that Richard was safely home from school and that the two of them would be going out the next evening, then kissed them each goodnight and crawled into bed to begin restlessly counting down the hours and minutes until her cousin's appearance.

At exactly 7:00 o'clock, Richard pulled his car into the driveway and rang the doorbell. Margie's whole body trembled as she answered the door and invited him in. She took a deep breath to calm her nerves as Richard eyed her up and down before entering. He sighed and shook his head as he stepped across the threshold. "Margie, I believe you're growing up at last," he observed.

Margie tilted her head, bemused. "I don't think you've ever called me by my real name before," she noted. "Sounds a little strange."

Richard smiled as he placed his hand at the small of her back and urged her through the doorway. "Chalk it up to your increased maturity."

Margie snorted. "Unfortunately, I'm still just me," she complained, as he shut the door behind them.

Richard shook his head. "No matter how you change on the outside, I hope you'll always be 'just you.'" He winked and tapped the end of her nose with his forefinger as he helped her into the car. Once again, Richard did not discuss with Margie her preference of destinations but merely headed toward Hollywood.

"Where are we going?" She suspected the question was futile.

"You'll see."

"You do like surprises, don't you!"

Richard smiled. "Yeah, I guess I do."

He parked the car and helped Margie out, then draped his arm across her shoulders and led her down Hollywood Boulevard. Margie was so taken with all the glitz that she was hardly aware of where they were headed until she detected some notable footprints in the concrete and looked up to behold the famous Grauman's Chinese Theater. It didn't matter what was playing; she was just thrilled to be there.

After the show, they stopped at a drive-in for a hamburger, then steered homeward. "Do you always sit clear over there when you're on a date?" Richard referred to the fact that Margie was leaving a wide berth between them. "C'mon over here and sit by me."

She hesitantly complied, and Richard placed his arm around her shoulders and pulled her close. He wasn't sure that the timing was right even yet but was no longer able to refrain from expressing his thoughts. "Just for the record," he said, "you know you have a standing offer of marriage from me."

Margie sighed wearily. "Richard . . ."

"I know! I know! We're cousins! But don't you get it, Margie? I simply don't care." Then, deciding to risk it all, he pressed on, "What about you? Is it really so important to you what other people think?"

"I don't know, Richard," she answered plaintively. "It just seems wrong."

"Hmph, not to me. To me it seems like the most 'not wrong' thing that we could do."

"Is it even legal?"

"It is in California."

Margie's eyebrows shot up. "You've checked?"

Richard shrugged. "Thought I might need to know someday. So the offer still stands, just in case you ever decide to consider it."

"But if we did get married," Margie reasoned, "we couldn't have children."

Richard took a deep breath, consciously calming his emotions. "Yeah, well, that's really not important to me, but I know it is to you. So, we could adopt. Probably not a whole dozen, though," he added in an attempt to lighten the mood. "Would you settle for three or four?" He hoped this would earn him a smile, but Margie was closer to tears. "Ah, don't worry about it, Kid. I'll always be yours, any way you'll have me."

Margie leaned her head against Richard's shoulder and wished, for the umpteenth time, that one of them had been born into a different family.

Richard didn't call Margie again for a few days; he was in a quandary over his career choice, as well as in a funk over the situation with his bedeviling cousin. Once again, he was berating himself for pressuring her prematurely. He had been in love with her for so long; it was hard to remember that she was only fifteen. After many hours of soul-searching, there seemed only one option, at least for the time being. He took care of the necessary preliminaries and then telephoned Margie.

"I need to tell you something. Are you going to be home for a little while?"

This had a familiar feel to it, and Margie wasn't sure she wanted to hear what Richard had to say. But she did want to see him. "Yeah, I'll be here."

"All right if I come over?"

"Of course."

A short while later, the doorbell rang, and Richard was ushered into the living room. He settled on the sofa–with Margie perched sideways a few feet away–and looked about him, fidgeting, finding it impossible to get comfortable. He finally leaned back and folded his arms. "I guess I'll just say it. I've signed up for the Air Force."

"You're leaving again?" Margie cried. "But you barely got home!"

"Yeah, well, there's no point in me sticking around here." He wanted to tell her that she had only herself to blame for his going, that it was because of her that he needed to escape. Instead, he attributed the decision to his wavering over career choices. "When I figure out what to do with the rest of my life, then maybe I'll stay put for awhile."

"How soon do you leave?" she asked mournfully.

"In a few days."

Margie's eyes began to tear. "And how long will you be gone this time?"

Richard paused. "A couple of years," he mumbled.

Margie bolted up from the sofa and walked to the wall of windows that looked out to the back yard, folding her arms in front of her as she gazed, unseeing, through the glass. "I'll be in college by then," she observed.

"Yeah, I know." Richard followed to stand behind her, his hands thrust into his pockets. "That's okay. You need to get away from home, come out from under your shelter. Maybe by the time I get back, you'll have a better idea about what you want." She turned to face him, and he looked at her with pleading, telling her with his eyes that what he wanted wasn't likely to change.

She got the message. "Richard . . ."

He nodded. "Yeah, I know. Well, we can at least write, can't we?"

She smiled and sniffled. "Yeah."

Chapter XI

During her senior year, Margie began dating a young man from church. Wade was one of the more attractive of her cohorts, not as tall as she would have liked, but with dark brown hair, piercing blue eyes, and a wide dazzling smile, as well as a sharp dresser. Margie had often admired his good looks, and even casually spoken to him on occasion, both at church and at school, but they had never really connected. Their romance began one Sunday evening when he unexpectedly asked to take her home from church, and Margie gladly accepted.

After making their way to Wade's little Chevrolet coupe, Margie slid into the passenger seat. It was a warm evening, and she rolled down her window in anticipation of the breeze that would be generated by the moving vehicle. Wade settled himself behind the steering wheel, started the engine, and pulled out of the parking lot, then glanced at Margie, a slightly puzzled expression on his handsome face. "I wonder why I've never noticed you before," he said. "I mean, I've noticed you, of course, but not noticed you."

Margie blushed. "I'm not exactly the type that stops cars!"

"Well, you flagged mine down. What I don't get is why it took me until now to put on the brakes!"

Margie chuckled with pleasure at the compliment. Wade must see something in her that was not visible to most of the young men of her acquaintance. She had dated off and on for the past three years, but boys didn't exactly line up at her door the way they did at Donna's. Those who did ask her out were usually several years her senior, and while it was true that she was ordinarily attracted to more mature men, it was gratifying to be appreciated by someone her own age.

"I suddenly realize that you're very cute," Wade continued.

Margie nearly choked over that one. "You're kidding, of course." She had no false notions about her appearance; she knew that she was no beauty. Nevertheless, it was pleasant–albeit embarrassing–to be so flattered, and she couldn't help but smile.

"Don't put yourself down like that! I mean it; I think you're cute."

"Thanks," muttered Margie.

"So, would you like to go to dinner some night?" he asked.

Margie didn't have to think twice. "Sure, that'd be fun."

"This Friday okay?"

"Friday's fine; what time?"

"I get off work at six, so we could go about seven. Or do you prefer to dine fashionably late?" he asked urbanely.

"Huh," Margie said, smiling. "I guess I'm always too hungry to become fashionable. Seven's okay."

Wade picked her up exactly on time the following Friday and drove straight to the restaurant that he had chosen beforehand, chatting amiably all the way. It was comfortable being with Wade; he made conversation easily, whereas tête-à-tête had never been Margie's strong point. The drive took about thirty minutes and when Wade brought the car to a halt, Margie noticed with dismay that they were parked in front of a seafood dining room. She wouldn't have minded not being consulted about her tastes, except for the fact that she despised fish. She supposed she could order the shrimp; that wouldn't be too bad as long as they brought plenty of cocktail sauce to drown it in. She certainly didn't want to destroy her chances so early in the game by complaining about his unfortunate choice.

After they were seated, Wade opened the menu in front of him and suggested, "They have really good abalone here."

Determined to keep her seafood aversion under wraps, she tried to make him believe that she had her heart set on the shrimp.

"Have you ever tasted abalone?" he asked.

Margie hesitantly shook her head.

"Then you've got to try it!" he insisted.

She grimaced. "Well, the problem is that I don't really like seafood."

"Oh, great!" he threw up his hands in mock despair. "Our first date and I've already blown it!"

"No! It's okay." She was mortified now that she had ruined everything. "I'll just have the shrimp."

But Wade was not to be disheartened. "Just try the abalone," he pleaded. "I think you'll be pleasantly surprised." Margie gave him a look that clearly expressed her doubt, but reluctantly acquiesced, and when her plate was set before her, she eyed its contents suspiciously. Fortunately, a cup of tartar sauce accompanied the meal, its solitary saving grace. Placing her napkin on her lap and taking a deep breath, she picked up her fork and plunged it into the sauce. When she had heaped on a generous amount, she then stabbed a small piece of fish and began to bring it to her mouth.

"You won't even taste the abalone drenched in that much

sauce!" Wade objected as Margie grimaced. That had been the whole idea. At the look on her face, Wade burst out laughing. "C'mon," he said, "be brave." He took the fork from her hand and reversed the size of the portions on it, then turned it toward her. Margie scrunched her eyes shut and obediently closed her teeth over the morsel, pulled it off the fork, and began gingerly chewing.

Her eyes popped open in surprise. "That's actually pretty good," she announced.

Wade shrugged and grinned. "Papa knows best." He then took his own napkin and, leaning across the small table, wiped some sauce from the corner of her mouth, an intimate gesture which pleased Margie immensely.

As they were saying goodnight at Margie's front door a couple of hours later, Wade took her hand in his and asked, "Is it all right if I call you again?"

Margie nodded and smiled. "Yeah, I'd like that." She had to admit that she'd had a good time. She simply needed to stop comparing every boy she met with Richard!

The following Monday, as Margie and her friends were eating their sack lunches around a table in the lunch room, Emily and Donna quietly announced that they planned to ditch school that afternoon and drive to the beach–Emily was one of the few of Margie's girlfriends lucky enough to own her own car.

"You want to come?" they asked.

"Oh, I can't," Margie answered in what she hoped was a regretful tone. "I have a trig test this afternoon."

"So make it up later" was their simple solution.

"No, I'd better not." The truth of the matter was that Margie didn't possess her friends' derring-do. She was too afraid of being caught by the truant officer and falling out of favor with her teachers; she prided herself on impeccable conduct and top-notch grades. Consequently, though she was comfortable with her straight-laced existence, she always had the niggling feeling that the more adventurous side of life, so expertly embraced by her friends, was passing her by.

Donna telephoned Margie that evening. "You should have come with us today!" she chided. "You'll never guess who was there!" Then, not able to wait for Margie's response, she supplied the answer, "Al and Jim and Wade. And Wade wanted to know where you were."

Margie couldn't help smiling to herself. "So, what did you tell him?" she asked.

"I told him that you were too chicken to skip class."

"Dooonna," Margie whined.

"Well, it's the truth, isn't it?"

"I told you I had a trig test."

"Yeah, yeah, yeah. Anyway, it was obvious that he was disappointed. I think he's got it bad for you. You're so lucky; he's only the most gorgeous boy at school! And guess what else! Al asked me out for Friday night. And Jim was acting pretty friendly with Emily."

Margie was excited at the news. What fun it would be if her two best friends started dating Wade's buddies–but only, of course, if she and Wade continued to see each other. She indeed hoped that would be the case. "We could have so many good times if all of us started doing things together," she exulted.

"Well, keep your fingers crossed. And pray I don't do something stupid on Friday night to scare him off!"

Margie guffawed. "You know all the boys are crazy about you, no matter what you do!"

"If that's true," Donna retorted, "then I suspect there's a

major flaw in their judgment, but who's complaining?"

After a lengthy discussion about what they should wear to school the next day, the girls closed their conversation with a "see you tomorrow." Margie finished up her homework, then went in search of her dad, knowing exactly where to find him. She happily cuddled up next to him on the sofa in the den to enjoy their weekly rendezvous in front of the television set watching *Bonanza.*

"Hi, Susie," he greeted her, using a pet name. "Homework all done?"

"Yeah."

"Just in time. Show's starting."

Grace never seemed to have time for such frippery, so it was always just the two of them, but Margie cherished every minute she could spend with George, even if it meant mindlessly staring at the "boob tube" together. She breathed in the familiar scent of Old Spice, one of the constants about her daddy that never failed to comfort, and slid her hand through his arm as she leaned her head against his shoulder.

Tonight, however, she couldn't concentrate. She gave up before the show was finished, kissed her dad goodnight, explaining that she couldn't keep her eyes open, then brushed her teeth, set her hair in pin curls, and put on her pajamas. As she turned out the light and crawled between the sheets, she reran the part of her conversation with Donna that spoke of Wade's "having it bad" for her. That thought would make for pleasant dreams, if she could ever get to sleep!

Chapter XII

The school lunch table, always a beehive of activity, became even more chaotic as it expanded to include Wade and his two friends. Wade always made it a point to arrive early enough to grab the chair next to Margie's, and it soon became apparent to the others in the group that they were "an item."

Before long, Wade was driving Margie home from school every afternoon on his way to work, and then stopping by her house again after closing up the small grocery store owned by his uncle. On the weekends, they tried out different restaurants–tacos and pizza were newly introduced novelties in southern California and were quickly adopted as favorites. They attended dances, went to the movies, joined other couples for beach parties, and enjoyed concerts and live theater, usually triple dating with their closest friends.

"Judy Garland will be at the Shrine next weekend! Do you want to go?" Margie had barely opened the front door when Wade burst into the entry and disgorged his exciting news.

"I love Judy Garland!" Margie could hardly contain herself. "Of course I want to go!"

"I'll call Al and Jim and see if they want to triple. Does it matter whether it's Friday or Saturday night? I'm not sure which I can get tickets for."

"Either night is fine. I love Judy Garland!"

He chuckled with pleasure at Margie's obvious excitement. "Yeah, so you said."

Wade wasn't really a music–nor a show biz–buff, but he knew how much Margie enjoyed that sort of thing, so he was feeling very pleased with himself at being able to offer her an evening of such high-caliber entertainment. He was willing, himself, to be semi-bored for a couple of hours just to please her. In fact, he'd have done almost anything to earn her favor. Margie, on the other hand, avoided as best she could any serious bent in their relationship. She had initially been swept away by his attentions, gaining the devotion of such an attractive and sought-after boyfriend had been quite a coup, and she continued to welcome his virtually constant companionship but knew instinctively that there was a distance to go before she was ready to make any kind of long-term commitment. She wondered what Richard would think of Wade, and the thought brought a smile to her lips. She doubted that Richard would think anyone was worthy of her–anyone but himself, that is.

"Well, I can't stay tonight." Wade went on. "I've got to go home and get some homework done. I just wanted to ask you about the Judy Garland concert. So I'll see you tomorrow." He gave her a quick kiss and left.

No sooner was he out the door than Margie ran to the telephone and dialed Donna's number.

"You'll never guess what!" she blurted out.

"Well, let's see. You're pregnant?" Donna quipped.

Margie giggled. "How did you know? Does it show already?"

"Well, I didn't want to say anything, but you are getting a

little thick around the middle."

"What? I am not! I haven't gained an ounce!" Margie was almost insulted.

"I'm just kidding. What's your big news?"

"Wade just asked me to the Shrine for a Judy Garland concert. He's going to phone Al and Jim, so you'll probably be getting a call. I'm so excited, I can't stand it! I wonder if Mom will let me get a new dress. Of course I'll probably break out in pimples and have ugly hair that night–uglier than usual, I mean. You can go, can't you? It's next weekend, Friday or Saturday; I'm not sure which."

"Of course I can go. Wild hippopotamuses couldn't keep me away!"

"What about objecting parents?"

"I'm sure it'll be okay."

"All right. Well, I've got to call Emily. So, just remember to act surprised when Al phones. See ya."

The same conversation was then repeated, with Emily as the recipient, before Margie finally settled down to homework and bed. In her dreams, she was on stage at the Shrine Auditorium, singing to an enormous crowd and altogether in her glory until someone in the audience shouted, "Your hair is ugly–uglier than usual!" Another voice joined in with, "Yeah, and you've got pimples!" Still another cried out, "How come you're so thick around the middle?" And the final indignity, "Hey, girl, you're in your underwear!" Margie burst into tears, fled from the stage, and woke up feeling repulsive and depressed.

Fortunately, when the anticipated evening arrived, it was indubitably Judy Garland on stage, and Margie's complexion and hairdo were insignificant details amidst a great mass of nameless humanity. Judy's countenance, on the other hand, was flawless, as was her performance. At its conclusion, Margie left the auditorium feeling exhilarated and, at the same time, testy. This type of evening always aroused within her a sense of discontentment which couldn't be expressed to anyone except perhaps Richard and which rendered her incapable of ordinary conversation. At such moments, her only desire was to be alone with her thoughts and dreams; she resented the intrusion of even her best friends.

Wade didn't have a lot of money–the wages earned at his after school job did little more than cover the cost of their dates and put gas in his car. But Margie was unaware of his sacrifices. It never occurred to her that her friends sometimes struggled in order to subsist in the high school milieu. She wasn't insensitive, just oblivious.

Over spring vacation, Margie's father, because he had perceived that Wade seldom, if ever, had the opportunity to participate in expensive frivolity, generously invited him to accompany Margie, Grace, and himself on an outing to Catalina Island.

They had planned to board the large ship that sailed over every morning and returned every night, but they arrived at the harbor too late–there was no more room on the transport. George approached a man sitting in a small open vessel–appropriately referred to as a "water taxi" (it afforded its passengers a little less space than a modest-sized car)–and asked about a round trip to the island. The man happily agreed, for a sum that George not-so-happily paid, and they were on their way, right in the wake of the ship, making for a very choppy ride. Margie had never been prone to motion sickness, so she thought it great fun. Wade, on the other hand, was slightly green by the time they reached their destination.

"Are you okay?" asked a concerned Margie, who thought it

quite commendable that he had, by sheer willpower, avoided feeding the fish along the way.

"I will be. Just give me a few minutes, or hours, maybe." Wade tried to offer an assuring grin but could only manage a grimace.

The day was disappointingly overcast, but the tourists didn't seem to notice. The island was teeming with bright colored shirts and bare legs. Once there, George treated his family to lunch–he had little sympathy for Wade's queasiness. George was a generous and sensitive man when it came to helping those who couldn't help themselves, but he believed that anyone could control the discomforts of their own body by practicing "mind over matter." Understandable, perhaps, since he had never been sick a day in his life–not even so much as a headache.

After seating themselves in the restaurant, Margie was brave enough to order the abalone without any prompting. Wade, however, did not follow suit, but settled for French fries and a 7-Up, the reason being obvious.

The next item on George's agenda was a submarine ride. Wade, though averse at this moment to boarding anything that traveled in or on water, couldn't admit that Margie was a "better man" than he, so he assured them all that he was completely recovered and had always wanted to see the inside of a submarine.

Margie had her own misgivings–her claustrophobia was sufficiently intense that she conscientiously avoided closed doors and tight spaces. Reluctant, however, to disappoint her father, she also denied her disinclination. It was obvious that George, wanting to insure a good time for everyone, had his heart set on this new adventure. Fortunately, the ride along the ocean floor was short and the tour of the vessel reasonably interesting; the young people both survived.

"What now?" Margie inquired of her dad.

"Now you and your mom get to indulge in your favorite pastime while Wade and I tag along behind. Try not to spend too much money." This last precaution was added facetiously; George basked in the opportunity to pamper his women.

"You know we never spend any money, Dad. Mom just writes on a little piece of paper and signs her name." This was a family joke of long standing and never failed to evoke a chuckle from George.

The foursome spent the rest of the day browsing little gift shops along the primary thoroughfare and collecting souvenirs. As the sun began to set, they made their way to the dock to be taxied back to the mainland. Wade again kept his stomach in tight rein, and Margie couldn't help but find humor in his discomfort, though she was too well bred to mention it. Nevertheless, her voice held a betraying hint of mirth as she tried to offer consoling words. "Is there anything I can do for you?" she asked. "I feel bad that you didn't get to have a real lunch. I think you've got me hooked on abalone."

Margie laughed over her inadvertent pun, while Wade, unavoidably visualizing the meal which Margie had so enthusiastically devoured, lunged toward the edge of the boat and hung his head over the side, as his churning stomach purged itself. A pale-faced Wade sheepishly returned to his seat, wiping his mouth with his handkerchief.

"Sorry," Margie offered, then pressed her lips together, trying to maintain her composure.

"You're laughing at me," accused Wade.

"No!" Margie giggled. "I'm sorry. Really, I'm sorry." She then looked away from him, hoping to hide her merriment. Wade was not fooled but was feeling too queasy to further object.

After returning to the Nelson house, Margie borrowed her parents' car to deliver Wade to his door. "So, have you been accepted at college yet?" he asked as soon as they were on their way.

"Yes, as a matter of fact." Margie was excited about her plans to attend the University of Colorado. College had been a dream of hers for as long as she could remember. "I just got my letter yesterday."

"When does school start there?"

"I'm going up the end of August to get moved into the dorm and take the entrance exams and do orientation. Classes start in September."

Wade was already beginning to feel the pain of separation. "I'm going to miss you." His soulful tone caused Margie to cringe inwardly. She had made a conscious effort to keep their relationship on the light side, knowing that college for her was an absolute and the chances of her subsequently staying true to Wade almost nil. "I've been planning this for a long time, Wade. It's just something I have to do."

He nodded. "Yeah, I know. Just don't go falling for some college man and forget all about me."

Margie was at a loss for words. Though she was pretty sure that Wade was not the one she wanted to spend the rest of her life with, the subject hadn't heretofore been openly discussed, and now he was making uncomfortable assumptions. She simply smiled and asked, "Are you all right now? Sorry we had such a bumpy ride on the boat."

"You wouldn't be trying to change the subject, would you?"

"No! I'm just . . . wondering if you're okay," she lied.

"Why don't you want to talk about us?"

He was backing her into a corner and she didn't like the sensation. Margie didn't know how to explain her feelings without hurting his. "Well," she said finally, "since there's no way for us to know what's going to happen to either one of us this next year, what's the use of talking about it? Besides, it's just possible that you'll be the one to meet someone and forget all about me!"

Wade huffed. "That's doubtful."

"But it's possible. Can't we just put things on hold for a while; see how we feel a year from now?

"If that's the best you can offer, I guess I have no choice."

Margie pulled the car over to the curb in front of Wade's house, turned off the key, and turned to face him. "Wade, please don't put all of this on me," she begged.

Wade sighed heavily; he was suddenly weary of the subject. "Okay. Will you just promise me one thing, that you'll at least give us a chance?"

Margie nodded. "I promise." She didn't, at this point, know exactly what it was she wanted, except to have this conversation over. "Don't be mad at me, okay?"

Wade forced a smile, but his eyes belied the effort. "I'm not mad." He leaned over and kissed her. "I'll see you tomorrow," he promised, then climbed out of the car and disappeared into his house.

The next two months were a whirlwind of activities for the senior class, with picnics, dances, parties, and, of course, final exams, as well as the signing of yearbooks and rehearsals for the commencement exercises. Margie was proud to be named valedictorian of her class and nervous to be presenting the graduation speech.

"You'll be fine," Donna assured her. "It's just like giving a talk at church."

"Oh, yeah, except for the thousand people in the audience," Margie countered, "not to mention all the high mucky mucks from the board of education!"

"Why should they matter; you'll never see 'em again."

"Well, there is such a thing as pride. I don't want to make a fool of myself in front of anybody, even if I won't ever see them again."

"Margie," Donna shook her head, "a lotta things you are–fool is not one of them!"

At 6:30 pm on the night of June 11, Margie stood in line with 500 high school seniors at one end of their football stadium as the band began to play Bach's "Marche Noble." She couldn't calm her butterflies as she slow-stepped to her place of honor on the impromptu stage opposite the bleachers where, among a few thousand spectators, her family had proudly seated themselves.

The colors were posted, the invocation offered, and the school song presented by the a cappella choir. It was then Margie's turn at the podium. Her mind went blank as she gazed out over the vast audience. Panic struck. She closed her eyes and reminded herself to breathe, then, "Dr. Garton, Dr. Heisner, Principal Hurlbert, distinguished guests, fellow students, friends, and families," she began. There was another pause as a smile slowly spread across Margie's face.

In a bold voice, she continued, "I feel it a great honor to stand before you today, representing the class of 1952." A happy cheer arose from the students. "Words cannot express the gratitude I feel for the privilege of receiving the quality of education that is offered at Westchester High School. The instructors here have been an inspiration to me. As they have imparted their wisdom and knowledge, I have been thrilled, agitated, entertained, and surprised but never disappointed. I applaud this faculty for their intellect, their ability, their sense of humor, and their concern for their students.

"I will never forget the excitement, as well as the apprehension, which we all experienced during those first few weeks as freshmen in high school. And now an unbelievable four years have passed. As we face the future with that same excitement and apprehension, may we always remember what we have been taught here, not only by our teachers, but by each other.

"One important thing that I have learned during these years is the fact that commitment will carry us further toward our destination than will talent. We students understand the meaning of commitment; otherwise we wouldn't be here today. So my challenge to all of us is that we enhance in the future what we have done in the past. Let us commit ourselves to becoming men and women of strong minds, great hearts, true faith, and ready hands. Let us be committed to our goals and refuse to settle for less than we can achieve. This will bring us success. Let us be committed to our obligations, no matter how onerous the task. This will strengthen our character. Let us be committed to our own personal standards. This will bring us the respect of others. Nothing we desire will ever be worth the compromising of our integrity. And let us be committed to our God. This will assure our ultimate happiness.

"As we now move on so that others may avail themselves of the opportunities which have been ours, may we reflect on our yesterdays with self-respect and gratitude and approach our tomorrows with resolution.

"Faculty members and fellow students, I appreciate the significant part which you have played in my preparation for future endeavors. You have forced me to work hard. You have inspired me to reach and grow intellectually and artistically. You have broadened and enriched my mind and enlarged my soul. And you have been my friends. For all of this, I thank you."

Margie beamed as the audience clapped their approval. Then, just as she was taking her seat, she noticed that her lunch room friends were arising en masse to offer a standing ovation. Chagrined, she lowered her eyes as a blush infused her cheeks. In the audience, Grace was slightly disapproving of their unseemly behavior–empathizing, no doubt, with Margie's obvious discomfort, but George thought it hilarious.

That night, Margie and Wade, along with Donna, Emily, and their "steadies," Al and Jim, enjoyed dinner at a sophisticated restaurant. They ran home and changed clothes for a lengthy marshmallow roast on the beach, where they were joined by several of their classmates. The festivities concluded with an early breakfast of bacon and pancakes at Donna's house (Margie was, by this time, seriously considering that tapeworm).

"I can't believe we're really out of high school," remarked Donna after the three girls had placed the food on the table and everyone was seated.

Margie concurred. "Some of those kids we may never see again. It makes me kind of sad, you know?"

"No more football games or junior proms," noted Emily wistfully. "Well, maybe for you, Margie, since you're going on to college. But for the rest of us, high school was it!"

"Okay, you guys," interjected Al. "I'm getting depressed."

"Yeah," added Jim. "After all, we've still got a couple of months before the old crowd will start breaking up."

They agreed that they should take advantage of the time left to them, and big plans were presently in the making. Their spirits rose as they discussed the onset of "those crazy, lazy, hazy days of summer" complete with happily anticipated picnics and beach parties.

Suddenly, Margie was reminded of the afternoon of Richard's graduation, how disappointed she had been when he had left with his friends. It was clear to her, at this moment, why his buddies had taken precedence over his family, and she silently chided herself for her childish jealousy, though still dismayed at the unfortunate outcome of his choice. But then, she had only been a child, so she supposed that her petulance was forgivable. Even so, if Richard were here now, she would have happily chosen an evening with him over her high school friends.

The remainder of June was indeed hazy, so quickly did it fly by. Before they knew it, Independence Day had arrived, the activities for which had been planned well in advance. Wade, along with Al and Jim, picked up Margie and her girlfriends and drove to Balboa Bay, the place to go. They left home early in the morning to arrive there while they could still find room to spread out their beach towels.

It was a matter of pride to tell your friends that you had swum across the bay, so that was the first thing Margie wanted to do. "Who's going to swim to the opposite side with me?" she challenged. But none of the others cared in the least about placing that particular feather in their cap, so Margie was on her own. While her friends watched, she stroked her way easily across the water, then turned to come back. About fifty feet offshore, she frantically began calling, "I've got a cramp! I don't think I can make it!" Her head disappeared below the surface, then reemerged, only to go under again, her arms flailing wildly.

Wade plunged into the bay, his heart pounding, fearful that he wouldn't reach her in time. His already powerful strokes were enhanced by the rush of adrenaline, and he pushed himself relentlessly to the limits of his strength. The other four watched anxiously, the girls close to tears, the boys nervously pacing the shoreline in case their help was needed. Nearby sunbathers, alerted by Margie's cries, were observing with some alarm as her head kept vanishing from view then reappearing. Would help reach her soon enough?

It seemed like forever before Wade finally reached what he had calculated to be the correct spot. He apprehensively raised his head to locate Margie's exact position and was first stunned and then outraged to discover her easily treading water and smiling at him. "I just wanted to see if you'd really try to save me."

Wade's frigid expression clearly conveyed his anger. "Don't you ever do anything like that to me again. I mean it!" With that, he turned and made his way back to shore with a non-contrite Margie paddling along behind. The interested spectators turned away, almost in disappointment, as the anticipated drama fell flat.

"What happened?" inquired Donna, wondering why the rescue attempt had been aborted and noticing the dour expression on Wade's face as he preceded Margie out of the water and sat down next to his buddies. Margie peevishly grabbed her towel and began drying off–a little more briskly than necessary, her countenance no sunnier than Wade's.

"Your friend here has a strange sense of humor," he answered, exhibiting his annoyance.

Margie spread her towel on the sand but remained standing, hands on hips. "Why are you so mad?" She deplored any type of conflict and would ordinarily avoid it at all costs, but there was no reason for him to be so offended by her little bit of teasing. "It was just a joke."

"Yeah, some joke!" It was clear that Wade planned to take his time in forgiving her, and she decided she couldn't care less. He was acting like a baby! Richard would never react this way; he probably would dunk her a couple of times as payback for duping him, then challenge her in a race back to shore, where they'd drop down on their towels laughing together over the whole thing. Then he'd shake his head and say something like, "Kiddo, you're a mischievous little imp, but I love ya anyway," or words to that effect.

Well, Wade could sulk all he wanted; it wasn't going to spoil her day. She sat on her towel, struck a glamorous (she hoped) pose, and simply ignored her surly boyfriend, focusing her attention solely on the other four, flirting openly with Al and Jim, and thus not exactly endearing herself to any of her companions, except maybe Al and Jim. They were immensely entertained and not in the least averse to reciprocating her overtures. By the time the group left to go home, Margie had succeeded in alienating not only Wade but Donna and Emily as well.

In spite of the awkwardness generated by the day's events, that evening, the six of them traveled together to the coliseum in Los Angeles to watch the annual display of fireworks–the plans had been made and the tickets bought; no backing out at this point. Wade drove his mom's car, with Margie leaving plenty of space between them in the front seat, while the other four crowded into the back.

Donna and Emily were uncharacteristically quiet during the first few miles of their trip, demonstrating their unwillingness to forgive too readily–they wanted it clearly understood that any repetition of that day's behavior would not be tolerated. Margie almost felt sorry for Al and Jim, who were ruefully doing their best to smooth things over. She'd worry about mending her own fences later on when she could apologize to her two best friends in private.

Wade's mood had lightened somewhat, but he still had a bit of an ax to grind. "Are you sure you wouldn't rather be with Al and Jim instead of me?" he inquired peevishly of Margie as they cruised along the dark highway.

"Well, you haven't exactly been a bundle of laughs today. I still don't know why you got so mad at me."

"You really scared me, Margie," he said, his tone more conciliatory. "I don't know what I'd do if anything happened to you."

Margie sighed, feeling slightly ashamed for the trick she had played (but only slightly–she still maintained that Wade had overreacted). Nevertheless, she apologized. "I'm sorry I made you mad. Can we just pretend that it never happened?"

"I'd like nothing better," he admitted.

Chapter XIII

Good-byes at the end of the summer were difficult. Margie knew that she was not head over heels and wished for Wade's sake that she were. He was a kind, sensitive boy, a great deal like Richard in the way that he cared for her: a true gentleman (unlike so many of his peers who struggled with the concept). She didn't know why she couldn't reciprocate his devotion; there was just something missing when they were together, something vital.

Margie was beside herself, endeavoring to ease Wade's distress over their parting but also eager to move on. "I'll be home for Thanksgiving," she assured him. "That's not very far away."

"I just might run up there in the meantime," he announced hopefully.

She smiled. "Okay. I'll look forward to it." That was a bold-faced lie, but to spare Wade's feelings and avoid any further display of emotion on his part, she allowed him to hope. Besides, who could tell? It might be that after a few weeks or months of absence, her heart would grow fonder.

Once on campus, however, Margie spent very little time focusing on what she'd left behind in California. In spite of what she considered to be her physical imperfections, it wasn't long before she was attracting a passable number of eligible young men. This was a mystery to her, but she wasn't complaining; it was the most exciting time of her life.

She had been fortunate in her assigned roommates. All of them freshmen, Sharon came from Florida, had a passion for music that matched Margie's own, and displayed exceptional virtuosity on the violin. Joan was from Arizona, working toward a degree in elementary education, and soon recognized as the most pragmatic of the four. Rachel, hailing from Las Vegas and majoring in the humanities–specifically the dating rituals of the male Homo sapiens–reminded Margie a great deal of her friend Donna, carefree and funny.

The four of them didn't seem like strangers, more like long-lost sisters brought together at last in happy reunion–fortuitous for Margie, who was unaccustomed to sharing her personal space so intimately. It might easily have been a disaster if her new friends had been less amiable.

Margie was in her element. Campus life was all that she had expected and more. The first few weeks of her independence erased any confusion she might have felt about her relationship with Wade. It was over, no question. But, true to spineless form, Margie hadn't bothered to advise him of the fact, and soon Wade was on his way to Colorado.

Having in mind a pleasant surprise, he didn't give notice of his intentions until he had arrived in Boulder, then telephoned from his motel room. Margie went into dither mode; she had dates for both Friday and Saturday nights that she would have to quickly–and regretfully–cancel in order to be with Wade.

On Friday night, they went to dinner in town, followed by a movie. Their conversation was stilted and generic, covering Wade's job and some night classes he was taking, Margie's studies (Wade listened out of courtesy), and their California friends–basically, who was dating and who was engaged. They all missed her and said to tell her "hi."

Wade held her hand during the movie and put his arm around her in the car on the way home, willing her to be the Margie of a month ago; but that Margie no longer existed. She was all but tapping her toes by the time they finally pulled up in front of her dorm. Wade walked her to the entrance, and she allowed him to kiss her goodnight, wishing that she weren't such a milquetoast. Well, he alone was to blame for her reticence; he had put her at a great disadvantage by taking time off from work and driving over a thousand miles to see her, unbidden, she might add. Still, the decent thing would be to come right out and tell him where she stood and get it over with, but not tonight.

The next morning, Wade and Margie visited the grocery store where Wade purchased the makings for a picnic lunch before they hiked into the nearby hills. Throwing a blanket onto the ground, Wade placed the sundry food items on it and sat down, with Margie settling a few feet away. She opened the loaf of bread and began to spread mayonnaise and stack on bologna, cheese, and lettuce.

"Pretty view from up here," Wade noted. He was dithering, so Margie merely nodded and waited for him to broach the subject that was obviously weighing on his mind. They helped themselves to sandwiches, potato chips, and pop and ate in silence for several minutes.

"What are your plans after school's out?" Wade finally ventured.

Margie sighed. "I'll be home for the summer, of course, and then I'm coming back here," she answered hesitantly. She knew that Wade had been hoping that her stint at college hadn't met whatever need had prompted her to attend in the first place.

"No chance that you'll change your mind?"

Margie couldn't look at him as she answered, "Pretty unlikely."

"Hmm. I guess that means you haven't missed me much."

Margie frowned in consternation. She couldn't remain noncommittal any longer. "Wade, I'm really sorry." She paused, trying to find the right words. "I'll always love you as a friend." Wade winced–the old "let's be friends" routine–and Margie went on, "But I don't think it can ever be anything more. I'm sorry."

Wade smiled wryly. "Evidently not as sorry as I am. So, have you met someone else?"

Margie shook her head. "No, it's not that."

"What then?"

She hesitated for several seconds, wishing this whole situation would just go away; how she hated confrontations! Then, it being impossible to avoid the issue, she continued, "I don't know how to say this any other way, but I'm just not in love with you, Wade. I wish I were. You're a wonderful person, and some girl will be lucky to get you. It just won't be me."

Wade nodded morosely. "Yeah, well, if you change your mind, you know where to find me." With that he stood and began to gather up their belongings. Margie folded the blanket and handed it to Wade, while she carried the sack with the leftovers.

Their tramp down the mountain was a quiet one, and when they arrived back at Margie's dorm, Wade handed her the blanket and stood awkwardly with his hands in his back pockets, looking anywhere but at her. "Well, I guess there's nothing more to say, is there?"

"Will I see you tomorrow?"

Wade finally made eye contact, looking as if he'd been slapped in the face. He snorted softly. "What's the point?" He shook his head. "I think I'll just head back to California tonight."

"Oh, Wade." Margie felt terrible. "I'm really, really sorry."

"Yeah, me, too." He sighed heavily. "I guess we'll see each other this summer. So, 'til then, have fun!" he gnarled sarcastically as he turned and walked away, leaving Margie in tears.

In May, Margie received word that Richard had extended his tour of duty for another six months. The news had not come from his own hand, however, but was included in a letter from Grace. Had he perhaps decided that Margie was right after all–that they should go their separate ways? Well, that was good! It was what they needed to do. So, why did she feel so desolate?

When Margie returned to California at the end of the school year, it was as if time had stood still in her old hometown, with the same people doing the same things–the exception being Jack, who had remained at the U of U and enrolled for the summer semester. Grace was still holding her club meetings and filling each day with twenty-five hours, and George continued to oversee the aircraft business and watch *Bonanza*. Margie found it comforting to slip into the old routine. She and her friends easily took up where they had left off, with the familiar round of beach parties and get-togethers.

Wade was now pursuing a petite little bottle-blonde who had moved in next door to Emily during Margie's absence. Brandi–was that even a name?–had been readily accepted into the tight group of friends, perhaps a tad more eagerly by the male contingent. It was inevitable that she and Margie would sooner or later cross paths, undoubtedly while the attractive young button buster was hanging on Wade's arm and his every word.

When the unavoidable encounter did take place, it wasn't as off-putting as Margie had anticipated. There were a few moments of initial awkwardness, but the girl was surprisingly warm and artless–she and Margie might never become friends, but there was no appreciable hostility. Wade exhibited some discomfort as the introductions were made–embarrassed, no doubt, by the speed with which he was mending his broken heart. Well, so much for true love. Still, Margie was glad for him.

One basic difference in the summer scenario was that many of her old companions were now holding down full-time jobs and were not available to frolic at any and all hours. Consequently, Margie's days were reasonably dull–a good book being her best ally–but at night, there were the customary confabs, though they usually ended at an earlier hour than had formerly been the custom; the newly established work day dictated a more plebeian routine. All in all, it was a pleasant summer, and though Margie looked forward to another year at CU, those simple precious days flew by much too rapidly.

Chapter XIV

In September, Margie returned to the university and resumed her music studies. She was living in an off-campus facility, which provided her with a bit more freedom than she had enjoyed the year before. At the new apartment, it was permissible for the girls (Sharon, Rachel, Joan, and she were once again sharing quarters) to occasionally invite in members of the opposite sex for dinner and socializing–a practice that had been strictly prohibited in the freshmen dorm.

One night early in December, as she was studying alone in her room–Sharon and Joan were in Denver for the weekend and Rachel was at the movies with a date–the front buzzer sounded. This was a common occurrence; friends often dropped by, at any hour, just to say hello. When she opened the door, however, she received an extremely pleasant shock.

"Richard! What in the world?" This was becoming a common phrase; his sudden appearances more often than not unexpected.

Her cousin grinned sheepishly. "Just couldn't stay away any longer, Kid." He lifted his hands in a sign of surrender. "I honestly tried, but it was no good."

Margie laughed joyously as she motioned him inside, her

eyes filling at the welcome sight of him. "Oh, Richard, I can't believe it's really you. It's so good to see you!" She wanted to hug him, but the complications of their relationship held her back; instead she folded her arms.

Richard had taken a hesitant step toward her, then disheartened by her unmistakable body language, stopped and nodded, a half smile on his lips, his own eyes glistening. "You too, Kid." He surveyed his surroundings while gaining control of his emotions. "So this is how school kids live these days. A little different than the places I remember."

"It's just been remodeled," she explained. Is this what it had all boiled down to? Two tongue-tied strangers standing here discussing her apartment? "Are you hungry?" she asked, not knowing what else to say. "We have a kitchen!"

Richard started to decline but reconsidered. "Yeah. Sounds good. What's on the menu?"

Margie led the way into the kitchen and busied herself at the refrigerator as Richard pulled a chair from the table, sat and crossed one ankle over the opposite knee, tilting back slightly.

"I could fix you a cheese sandwich and a bowl of soup," she offered.

"Reminds me of home. That'd be great."

"So what's going on with you?" Margie asked as she pulled the needed pans from the cupboard and began preparing the simple snack. "Are you back in California?" This was inane! What had happened to their easy conversations of the past? They'd never before been at a loss for words.

"Yeah," answered Richard. "For the time being, at least."

"You haven't written forever! I had to hear the news from Mom about your staying in for another six months." Did that sound critical?

Richard lowered the front legs of his chair and leaned forward, resting his elbows on his thighs and clasping his hands, suddenly solemn. "I know. I've been trying to do what you wanted and back off."

Margie turned to face him. "You know it's not what I want," she objected, "it's just what I think is best. But I didn't expect you to altogether disappear." She wasn't sure what she had expected. Would there ever be an end to this constant turmoil that enshrouded their friendship?

A wry grin lifted the corners of his mouth. "Didn't work at any rate." He sat back, shrugged, and went on. "Anyway, I'm out of the Air Force now and looking for a job. I've sent out a few résumés and am just waiting to be called in for an interview. So I decided to take advantage of what time I have and come see you before I perish from loneliness."

Margie rolled her eyes. "I'll bet you say that to all the girls."

The offhand comment earned her a wry glance. "You know better than that, Kiddo. There are no other girls."

Margie couldn't help but smile as she put the food on the table and took a seat opposite Richard. She should object to his flattering words–put a stop to his absurd promulgations–but couldn't deprive herself, just yet, of the pleasant emotions that his silly palaver generated. He quickly ate his meal, then sat back and studied Margie's face for a few moments, his eyes twinkling. "You're prettier than ever, I think."

Margie chortled. "Richard, I've never been pretty, and you know it."

"You've always been pretty to me," he disagreed.

That brought a blush to her cheek. "How long are you in town for?"

"Just a couple of days. I expect to get a phone call any time now."

"So you'll be in California this summer?"

"Plan to."

"Will I get to see you?"

"What do you think?"

Margie smiled and lowered her eyes. "I've missed you."

"Music to my ears, Kiddo." He reached across the table and took her hand. "It's getting late; I'd better head for the hotel so you can get your beauty rest, not that you need it!" Richard rose from the table and pulled Margie to her feet. "What time are your classes tomorrow? When will you be free?" Margie wrote out her schedule, and they set up a time for him to come by her apartment the next day. He draped his arm around her shoulders, refusing to curb his natural inclination any longer, and lead her to the front door, arriving just as Rachel burst through it after bidding her date a hasty farewell. "Longest night of my life!" she complained. "Remind me never to accept a blind date again–ever!" Then cocking her head at Richard, she exclaimed, "My, my, Margie's been holding out on us." Richard smiled and introduced himself.

"Close cousins or kissing cousins?" Rachel wondered aloud, coquettishly raising her eyebrows.

"Close, very close," was Richard's enigmatic reply.

"Hmm." Rachel placed her hands loosely on her hips and squinted her eyes. "That could mean a lot of things." She studied Margie's blank expression, then looked back at Richard, clearly hoping for a more definitive answer. Receiving no enlightenment from either quarter, she shrugged, turned toward the bedroom, and wiggled her fingers. "Well, nighty night for now. Nice to meet you, Richard."

Richard chuckled, waited until she was out of earshot, then asked, "She always that intrepid?"

"Pretty much, but I think she was showing off a little for your benefit."

Richard turned toward Margie then and took both her hands in his. He longed to pour out his heart to her–try once again to break down her defenses. Instead, he leaned forward and placed a kiss on her forehead. "See you tomorrow, Kid."

Margie spent another sleepless night occupied by thoughts of Richard. Would her torment never end? Was it even possible that she could someday find a man who could make her happy? A man who wasn't her cousin?

The next day, Richard arrived at Margie's door at the prescribed hour but with disappointing news. "I'm afraid we'll have to postpone our date. I just got a call from Mom. North American phoned and they want me to come in for an interview tomorrow afternoon. I'll have to drive all night to get there." He uttered a sigh of frustration. "I was hoping we'd get a chance to talk. There are things I want to say . . ." he held up a hand to halt her objections as she opened her mouth to speak. "I know you don't want to hear this, but nothing's changed. I'm still crazy about you, Kid." He paused, judging Margie's reaction. She merely nodded, teary eyed. He was about to continue but thought better of it, deciding that extra pressure would not work to his benefit. "Well, I've gotta get going," he said. "Keep me in your happy thoughts." He placed his hand at the back of her neck, pulled her close, and kissed her on the lips. "See ya later, Kid."

Margie wondered how she would ever become immune to Richard's onslaughts and trying to convince herself that it was time that she must.

Chapter XV

Margie was sitting at a study table in the library a few days later, absorbed in her research for an English paper due in one week, when a tall, good-looking student pulled out the chair next to her. "Anyone sitting here?" he asked softly.

Margie smiled up at him, shook her head, and resumed her reading.

He seated himself, then noted, "You're in my geometry class, aren't you!" Others at the table glanced up at him as he spoke. "Sorry," he said to everyone in general, apologetic for disturbing their concentration.

Margie examined the young man's face but failed to place it. There were approximately thirty students in her geometry class, all of them, with her one exception, being male. "I'm not sure," she whispered. "I might be; I do have a ten o'clock geometry class with Dr. Dean."

"Yeah," his expression brightened. "Pretty hard to miss you in there. You're the only bright spot in the class."

Margie smiled in pleasure, while disparaging looks were once more sent their way from their tablemates.

"Sorry again," he whispered. Then, turning to Margie and lowering his voice another notch, "How long are you going to be studying here? Want to get a hamburger at the Student Union when you're through?"

Margie shrugged. "Okay. I'm about done. Just a few more minutes."

Half an hour later, they were en route along the path to the Union building. Her new friend introduced himself as Leigh Monroe, a fellow sophomore, and asked, "Is this your first year at CU?

"No, I was here last year. How about you?"

"Started out at Pasadena City; transferred here this fall."

"So, you're from California?" Margie's eyebrows rose in delight.

"Yeah."

"So am I!"

"I know," was his unexpected reply.

Margie gave him a dubious look. "How would you know that?"

"Well, I have a confession to make. Geometry isn't the first time I've seen you. I heard you sing in California a couple of years ago at a dance. Pretty surprising to find you here in one of my classes."

Margie was astounded and highly flattered. She'd never thought of herself as "memorable" by any stretch of the imagination. She was being unexpectedly swept off her feet, and it was a nice feeling.

"I can't believe you've heard me sing!" she said.

"You've got a great voice. So, is that your major?"

"Yes, actually, it is. Although I don't know if I'll ever make it through." Margie grimaced. "They say it takes five years to graduate with a degree in music because of all the classes you have to take."

"Oh, you'll make it!"

Margie shrugged. She hesitated to admit that, at this point, a degree was not her top priority. Much as she loved music, and especially singing, she had in the last couple of days decided that the only way to solve the dilemma with Richard was to find herself a husband, and the sooner the better. Surely there was someone, somewhere, who could help her overcome her obsession with her cousin. "So what are you majoring in?" she asked, returning her mind to the conversation at hand.

"I haven't really decided yet. I'd like to study art, but there's not much future in that. So I'll probably go for a degree in architecture. That's the next best thing."

"You're an artist?" Margie was intrigued. She had taken a few art classes in high school, enough to know that it was a real gift–one with which she hadn't been blessed–to put onto paper or canvas anything even vaguely recognizable.

"I like to think I am," he admitted. "In fact, my fraternity has asked me to do our sculpture for the Snow Carnival next week. So, if you want to drop by and take a look, you can tell me if I'm any good."

Margie rolled her eyes. "You must be good or they wouldn't have asked you."

Leigh laughed. "Okay, then, I guess I just want you to come by and see it when it's done."

"Oh, I definitely will do that."

By this time they had reached their destination and, as usual, the noise level dampened any attempt at conversation. Still, Margie was enthralled. Leigh was handsome and charming, obviously talented, and on the upward track.

After finishing their hamburgers, they made their way up the hill to Margie's apartment. "Thanks for dinner," she said as they approached her door. "I had a really good time."

"Yeah, me, too. We'll have to do it again." Leigh waved.

Margie rushed inside to tell her roommates all about her latest conquest–did she dare hope that that's what it was?

"Is he cute?" Sharon wanted to know.

Margie's eyes sparkled. "He's really, really cute! And about six foot four, with blonde hair and brown eyes! And he's an artist! Oooh, I think I'm in love!"

"Is he rich?" queried Joan, ever the practical one.

"I don't know. I don't care. What difference does it make? He's gooorgeous!"

"Wouldn't hurt if he was rich, too!" noted Joan.

"Oh, you guys! Anyway, if he doesn't call me, I'll die!" She fell histrionically onto the bed as if in the last throes of mortality.

"Hmm." Rachel leaned over the "dead" body, pretending to feel for a pulse, then shaking her head in mock despair. "Nothing! Oh, well," her tone brightened, "life goes on; who wants to go for some ice cream?"

Chapter XVI

It seemed that Margie had, indeed, made a conquest. Leigh began telephoning every night, even after walking her home from class each day. Their communications were lengthy and often inane; Leigh was an entertaining, if intellectually shallow, conversationalist, and Margie was thoroughly amused.

They occasionally took in a movie or went out for a hamburger, but Margie could not persuade Leigh to accompany her to any of the concerts that she so thoroughly enjoyed–classical music was beyond his ken. Still, there was undeniably some kind of chemistry between them, and she was completely carried away.

Finally, it was announced that the snow-sculpting contest was in full sway. Margie strolled through the twenty or so entries, planning her route so as to end up at Leigh's fanciful rendering of a Colorado State University Ram and a CU Buffalo trying to sing in harmony, "the most impossible thing ever." Leigh stood close by, guarding his contribution.

"This is amazing," Margie acknowledged. "You are really good!"

"Ah, shucks," he hung his head in mock embarrassment.

"And you know it, don't you!" she laughed.

"Well, I don't like to brag, but there's a rumor going around that I might take first place."

Margie surprised herself–and Leigh–by throwing her arms around his neck and giving him a hug. "That's wonderful!" She drew back, blushing over her bold display of emotion. "Sorry," she giggled in chagrin.

Leigh had been taken unaware but did not look displeased. "Don't apologize. I'm not complaining. Of course, it hasn't happened yet," he said. "But, if it does, you're welcome to congratulate me again!"

"Well," said Margie, anxious to change the subject, "I guess I'd better get home. I hope you win." Waving her hand she walked back through the snow to her apartment, thinking all the way about this exciting new development in her life. There was no denying the attraction she felt toward Leigh; he had a personal magnetism that was almost impossible to resist, and she sensed that he was equally drawn to her. He didn't, of course, possess Richard's confidence or maturity. He wasn't as prone to accept responsibility or as concerned over Margie's comfort and well-being; he was more like an overgrown kid who, himself, needed protection and guidance. But then, Leigh was much younger than Richard; maybe in time. And, if not, how bad could it be?

Margie had, by this time, reached her building. "Hey, you guys," she called out as she entered.

A voice answered from one of the bedrooms, "We're in here," and Margie followed the sound to discover her roommates sitting on a bed, sharing a bag of potato chips. "What's up?" asked Joan.

Margie removed her coat and gloves and laid them across the back of a chair, then joined her friends on the bed, dipping her hand into the almost empty bag. "You guys have got to see Leigh's sculpture. It's so good! He's probably going to win first place."

"Spoken like a true critic!" teased Rachel.

"No! Really! It's incredible."

"Okay, we'll go take a look tomorrow," Rachel acquiesced. "By the way, are you two going to see each other over the Christmas holidays?"

"I hope so. But he does live a couple of hours away, so I don't know if he'll want to drive that far."

"No distance is too far when you're in looove," crooned Rachel, clasping her hands in front of her and batting her eyelashes.

"Well, he hasn't exactly said anything about looove yet," Margie demurred.

"Oh, but he will," Rachel assured her. "It's only written all over his face every time he looks at you!" The other girls expressed their accord.

Margie grinned. "Really?"

"Oh, listen to you. You know very well he's crazy about you."

Margie was pleased to receive this confirmation, along with the evident approval of her roommates. They seemed as anxious as she to facilitate the progress of this romance.

Christmas break was soon a reality, and Margie excitedly packed a couple of bags and obtained a ride with some of her friends to the Denver airport. She loved school, but it was always nice to go home, to the place where everyone had known her forever and understood who she really was.

Margie's parents were eager to meet this new love interest of which they had heard so much via her letters home, and Leigh managed the drive to their Westchester house on more than one occasion during the break from school. George found him to be good-natured company, and Grace was more than pleased with his abilities–she had always wanted an artist in the family.

There was the usual banquet at the Nelson home on Christmas Eve, during which Margie avoided any private conversation with Richard. She wasn't yet ready to reveal to him the details of her blossoming romance. He, in turn, was suspicious of her uncommon reticence but left it unchallenged, thinking it best to let her work through whatever was occupying her mind. Grandma, ever vigilant, noticed the coolness between them and expected that her long-held fears were about to be realized: One of them, and possibly both, was about to suffer a devastating hurt.

On New Year's Eve, Leigh accompanied Margie to the celebration at her church. He was an average dancer, nothing fancy but adequate, a slight disappointment to Margie, who preferred a little more flamboyance. She couldn't help but be reminded of the same dance four years ago, when Richard had suddenly appeared and rescued her from an evening of boredom. That was also the beginning of all of her wretched torment, when she finally understood Richard's true feelings toward her. She wondered what her cousin was doing tonight and if he was remembering as well.

Richard was, indeed, remembering and brooding. He was aware that Margie had a date and suspected, in view of her behavior at the family dinner, that it might be more than casual. Being in no mood himself to celebrate, he had stayed at home and fretfully thumped away on the piano. There was no humor in tonight's performance, no silly innovations. If the keys were talking, the story they told was one of frustration, regret, and even anger. Then, unable to calm his restlessness, Richard took a solitary walk as he mulled over the possibility that Margie might be falling in love–but not with him.

"So, how serious are you two?" Grace asked Margie the next morning.

"Well, we haven't known each other very long, Mom, but we've spent a lot of time together, and I think he might be the one."

"Is he a member of our church?" To Grace, this was an important consideration.

"Yeah." Margie drew out the word.

"But?" queried Grace.

"Well, I don't think he goes very often," Margie admitted. "But I'm sure he'd go with me, if we were married."

A worried expression clouded Grace's features. "Just don't rush into anything," she warned.

But Margie was possessed by an urgency to have her future settled. Marriage to Leigh would put an end to the thoughts of Richard that relentlessly inundated her consciousness. If things had been different, but there was no use torturing herself with useless "what ifs." Since a future with Richard was out of the question, she was convinced that Leigh was her best chance for happiness. When he proposed the following May, her answer was an unequivocal "yes!" The wedding was set for sometime in November.

My very dearest Richard,

Writing this letter is the hardest thing I've ever had to do. I realize that I should be telling you these things face to face, but I can't put this off until I see you again (besides, I'm a chicken at heart).

First of all, just let me confirm what you must already know: that you are so much more to me than just my dear cousin. No one could possibly replace you in my heart. Please remember that as you read on.

I know that I have caused you untold frustration over the years. I am so sorry for that. Blame it on my immaturity, my self-centeredness, my lack of consideration, but never on a deficiency of my love for you. You are my knight in shining armor, and this distressed maiden is unworthy of you in every way.

You have been unbelievably patient with me for so long. It's hard to believe that, for all of these years, you've continued to put up with my self-serving vacillations (always encouraging your attentions, too weak to let you go, yet never brave enough to abandon my own fears). And still, after all is said and done, I can't seem to overcome my hang-ups over the fact of our kinship. Oh, Richard, if only . . . if only.

Please forgive me for what I'm about to tell you (as well as for all of my other multitudinous wrongs). I've met someone at school, and we are getting married (I think you probably suspected that something was going on at Christmas time). He's a good man. My greatest fear is that I will always measure him against you, and no one can stand up to that kind of comparison.

I don't want this to be good-bye. A future without you would be bleak indeed. I have no idea what's appropriate at this point, but I hope you will always be my very dear friend (that sounds trite, doesn't it?). I guess I'm at a loss here, so I'll quit while I'm behind.

I didn't want you to hear this first from Mom; that would be just one more unforgivable deed on my part. I hope that by the time the wedding takes place (November), you will have realized that I was never worth all of the trouble I caused you.

It would be inane, at this point, for me to ask for your blessing, but please come to the wedding and at least wish me

well, and please, please forgive me.
Margie

Richard accepted the unwelcome communication quietly. Although he had tenaciously held onto a glimmer of hope for all of these years, he supposed that, realistically, he had never expected things to turn out in any other way. Nevertheless, he was heartbroken.

Grace determined that her only daughter's wedding would be the social event of the year–at least among her own acquaintances–and dragged Margie through every bridal shop in Beverly Hills that summer looking for just the right gown. Finally, they agreed on a full-skirted, tight-bodiced creation of imported lace and tulle, with plentiful pearls and beads attached throughout. Margie was amazed that her mother would spend $450 for something that would only be worn once, but Grace was obviously in her element, and Margie gladly followed her lead.

The countless preparations were managed with Grace's usual aplomb, requiring very little input from Margie, and the latter was happy to spend the hours with her future bridegroom while her mother saw to the wedding arrangements. Margie didn't really care about the intricacies of the event; she merely wanted it over with so that she could get on with the business of her "real life": having babies and living "happily ever after."

The anticipated day dawned in clear perfection. It was a short drive to Margie's church and, at the conclusion of a simple ceremony, she and Leigh immediately departed for the reception to be held in the Nelsons' spacious home. Over 400 guests made their appearance throughout the afternoon, among whom, of course, was Margie's Aunt Vera and cousin

Richard. Margie felt a lump in her throat as Richard approached. How dare he look so appealing on her wedding day? Nevertheless, she forced a smile as he took her hand in his.

"So, Kid, you went and did it," he said kindly, forcing a note of gaiety.

Margie nodded. "Yeah, I did."

"By the way," he asked sotto voce, "does your new husband know how many kids you want?"

Margie laughed. "Yeah, I thought I'd better let him in on that."

"And he agreed?" Richard raised his eyebrows in mock surprise. "He must be a better man than I!"

Margie shook her head, her eyes suddenly plaintive. "There's no such thing, Richard," she softly assured him.

Richard smiled, somewhat ruefully. "Well, be happy, Kiddo. Keep me in your . . ." he began, but then recognized the untimeliness of the familiar phrase. "Just be happy," he concluded. As Richard leaned forward to kiss Margie on the cheek, the definite odor of alcohol assailed her senses. She pulled back and frowned at him. "Richard?"

Understanding her reaction, he shrugged. "I had to do something to get through this night."

As Richard walked away, Leigh leaned over to Margie and asked, "Richard got a problem?"

Margie shook her head. "I don't know. I hope not."

Chapter XVII

After a three-day honeymoon in Las Vegas–compliments of Margie's father–the newlyweds returned to California and moved their belongings into an apartment in Hawthorne, close to the aircraft company where Margie's father served as vice president. George had, in blatant defiance of company policy regarding nepotism, supplied both Leigh and Margie with employment.

Though Margie appreciated what her father had done for her and was grateful for the much needed extra paycheck, she despised the day-to-day drudgery of rising at 6:30 a.m. to arrive at the job by eight o'clock; she detested the smoke-filled office that left her hair and clothes smelling foul; she abhorred the boredom of filing endless paper work and answering telephones that never quit ringing. She merely wanted to stay home and raise babies.

A little over a year passed, with Margie hoping each month to be pregnant, and each month reaping disappointment; she began to despair of ever realizing her most cherished dream. Leigh, on the other hand, seemed less concerned over her vexation and more concerned about the paycheck she was bringing in. He pretended to go along with her fanciful ideas about a large family, but in reality, preferred that they didn't come to fruition. Margie resented his comme ci, comme ça attitude but felt she couldn't complain. Leigh was working hard in a profession for which he was ill suited and offered him little satisfaction; she wasn't the only one not living her dream.

In addition to the troubles plaguing her own household, Margie was worried about Richard. Word through the grapevine was that he was drinking. Margie couldn't understand how he could even be tempted in that direction after what had happened to his father. Of course, according to Vera, Richard was, so far, only an occasional drinker; it wasn't like he was a drunk, per se. But possibly his dad had started out that way as well. Margie shuddered to think that Richard might follow suit. It made her own problems seem trifling in comparison. Still, it was hard to imagine that she may never have the babies she longed for.

After fourteen months of dashed hopes, Margie awoke one morning feeling like she had the worst case of flu in the history of mankind and gleefully realized that her fear of perpetual infertility could be banished. Leigh smiled at her news. "That's great, Hon," he said, putting his arms around her. "I know how much you want a baby."

"And what about you?" she asked. "Don't you want a baby?"

"Yeah. Of course I do," he assured her. But that night, he couldn't sleep, worrying about the added responsibilities of a growing family. Children didn't come cheap and didn't raise cheap. And he didn't know how he could make that kind of money materialize. Well, one good thing: When Margie realized that she wasn't just playing dolls, she'd undoubtedly give up her ridiculous notion of twelve children.

As the pregnancy progressed, Margie took a portion of each weekly paycheck and bought some small item that the new arrival would need. She hoped, in this way, that Leigh wouldn't notice so much the cumulative amount that must necessarily be spent. But then, why should he? He was basically clueless when it came to the household budget; he left that entirely up to Margie's administrative skills. His contribution to home management was merely to grumble because they never had any money and to somehow blame his wife for the deficiency. It seemed that all he thought about these days was the tight money situation, bemoaning the fact that it would soon become obligatory for Margie to quit working, and then what would they do?

This concern over finances was something of an adjustment for Margie, who had never before had to worry about how her needs would be met. It was a rather uncomfortable experience to suddenly find herself morphed into the responsible adult. For she was, by this time, beginning to realize that her husband had in some unspecified way become her first child. Had she inadvertently assumed the role as his emotional caretaker, or had it been forced upon her? She couldn't help but compare Leigh with her own father, who was in her estimation a perfect example of true manhood. He figured out the hard stuff, made the difficult decisions, and looked for ways to make Grace's life a little easier. In other words, he was an authentic gentleman–like Richard. In addition, Margie's earlier relationship with Wade had done nothing to dispel her expectation that all men conformed to that mold. Consequently, she was unhappily surprised to find herself taking on the more assertive role in her marriage.

Notwithstanding, Margie's days, once she had extricated herself from the loathsome office job, were spent in happy expectancy: cleaning house, cooking meals, and sewing baby clothes, which she folded and unfolded over and over again, anticipating the time when a tiny body would fill them.

In the evenings, she and Leigh would watch *Father Knows Best*, *The Lucy Show*, and other favorite sitcoms on an old television set that her parents had discarded. They almost never went out; Margie kept hoping that Leigh would show some sensitivity to her need for an occasional adventure–even a short ride in the car–but he preferred spending their nights at home and saw no reason why she shouldn't as well. Then she would berate herself for being so egocentric. She knew that he was tired after working all day; she shouldn't begrudge him some quiet time at home.

One afternoon in August, the doorbell rang. Margie answered it, expecting to see an unwelcome salesman and preparing in her mind a quick rejection, but to her great joy, she found her cousin leaning against the door jam.

"Richard!" she cried in delight. "What a surprise! C'mon in!" She could hardly contain her elation over his unexpected visit as she stood back and allowed him to enter. "Have a seat," she offered as she closed the door behind him.

"I can't stay long," he said as he lowered himself onto the couch and Margie settled in an adjacent chair. "I had a dentist appointment in Inglewood, so thought I'd drop by on my way back to work. How are you doing?" He gestured toward her increased girth. "You've put on a little weight since I last saw you!"

"Gee! Nice of you to notice!" Margie replied, rolling her eyes.

Richard chuckled. "Kiddo, on you it looks good! Seriously, though, how are you? Is everything going okay?"

Margie looked down at her hands. "Yeah."

Richard paused, considering her answer. "Not too convincing," he said with some concern.

Margie smiled. "No, I'm fine really."

"I hear a 'however' in there somewhere," Richard observed.

"You're not going to let it go, are you?"

Richard shook his head. "Not until I find out what's wrong."

Margie sighed. "It's just that marriage is different from what I expected. I guess that's stupid, isn't it?; it's probably not what anyone expects.

"Different how?" Richard asked, distress obvious in his voice.

Margie hesitated to elaborate her concerns, but having someone in whom she could comfortably confide made it impossible to hold back. "It's just that I never wanted to be the boss," she admitted.

"Ah," Richard nodded. "Well, you've got to realize that you're a strong person. That's pretty intimidating to a lot of men."

"It never intimidated you."

"No, but then I'm not 'a lot of men.'"

"Huh," Margie huffed softly, "that's for sure. I think you were transported here from another planet. Are you, by any chance, vulnerable to kryptonite?"

He chuckled. "No, just to head-strong independent women."

Margie looked at him askance. "Am I really like that?"

"It's not necessarily a bad thing. You'll probably accomplish great objectives during your lifetime, and I'll be the one saying, 'I knew you when.'"

"Oh, Richard, you've always thought I was more and better than I really am."

Richard shook his head. "Not so, Kiddo. Someday you'll realize that. I just wish there were something I could do to fix things for you right now."

Margie hesitated, wondering if she should say what was on her mind, considering if she had any right. Then, throwing caution to the wind, she asked, "What about you? Do you need someone to fix things?"

Richard's eyebrows rose. "What's that supposed to mean?"

Margie looked at her hands, folded in her lap. "Your mom says you're drinking."

"Pfff. She calls that drinking? What my dad did was 'drinking.' I just have a few now and then."

"But why? Why drink at all?"

Richard looked at her, almost accusingly. "My nights get pretty lonely, Kiddo."

Margie lowered her eyes. She didn't know how to respond. "I worry about you, Richard."

"Nah. You know me; I always land on my feet." The look in his eyes negated the easily spoken words.

"So you say. Just, please, take care of yourself."

"Sure thing, Kid. I always look out for number one." He stood, reluctant to go. "Well, I'd better get back to work." He took Margie's hands and kissed her on the cheek. "You know I'm just a phone call away."

Margie nodded. "I know."

Chapter XVIII

In October, Margie delivered a healthy baby boy whom she and Leigh named Gregg and who immediately brought to the forefront Margie's total lack of experience with infants. She had done a small amount of babysitting during high school, but because of her mom's paranoia concerning neighbors with whom she was not well acquainted–she fretted constantly about someone harming her innocent daughter–Margie's tending career was short-lived.

After two days in the hospital, Margie arrived home full of zeal concerning her new role and unrealistic expectations concerning her newborn. At about midnight on that first night home, after listening to her small son scream for approximately three hours, she called Grace.

"He just keeps crying," she sobbed, giving competition to the howling of her offspring. "I don't know what's wrong! I've changed him and fed him and he just won't stop!"

"Would you like me to come over?" asked her mother calmly.

"Do you mind?" Margie pleaded.

"I'll be right there."

Twenty wail-filled minutes later, there was a knock at the

door. Leigh answered and showed Grace into the bedroom.

"Do you want me to take him for awhile, so you can rest?"

"That would be great," replied an exhausted and very relieved Margie.

Amazingly, as soon as Grace took the child, his sobs subsided–a great blow to Margie's pride–and the rest of the night was spent peacefully, Margie's slumber only interrupted by the infant's feeding times.

In spite of the rocky beginning, Margie soon adapted and began to revel in the joys of young "mommy-hood." It wasn't long before she was yearning for another addition to their household–Leigh's prediction that she would ultimately abandon the idea of a large family thus becoming one more indication of how little he really knew her.

Leigh had, meanwhile, changed employment. He was still working in the aircraft industry but at a different company with a higher level, better paying position. The timing seemed expedient to continue working toward their–or rather her–goal.

They were also looking forward to purchasing their first home, a modest three-bedroom stucco located on a corner lot in Encino, closer to Leigh's new job. It had a large fenced yard–perfect for keeping little bodies occupied, entertained, and safe from traffic–complete with covered patio and a mature shade tree. On the day that they closed escrow, Margie confirmed with the doctor her suspicion that she was again pregnant. Needless to say, she was elated.

Leigh was more at ease concerning the preparation and arrival of their second child. The slight alleviation of financial strain had done wonders for his attitude; he was behaving more like the man Margie had fallen in love with: good-natured and communicative, even jovial now and then. He also began to take her on an occasional evening out. Of course, Greggie was their constant companion on these excursions–babysitters charged twenty-five cents an hour, to Leigh an unnecessary expense–but Margie didn't mind bringing along their little "third wheel." He was, for the most part, cheerful and well behaved.

"So, are you happy about another baby?" Margie asked one night after they had gone to bed, willing her husband to be as pleased as she was. It had been an exceptional evening, with dinner at their favorite restaurant, followed by a movie that Margie had been begging to see; it had felt like old times–like the carefree times of their courtship.

Leigh placed his arm around her shoulders and squeezed. "If you're happy, I'm happy."

"But I want you to be happy all on your own," she objected.

"Sure I'm happy. Junior needs a little playmate."

Margie sighed. "Why don't you ever call Greggie by his name?" Her annoyance over this continual slight was evident in her tone of voice.

"Ah, Margie, don't pick a fight."

"I don't want to fight; I just want to know why you can't say his name!"

Leigh withdrew his arm from her shoulders and folded it with the other one across his chest. "I can say his name," he announced with annoyance. "Greggie! Are you satisfied now?"

Margie rolled out of bed and walked to the nursery, where she gazed at the infant she adored, while Leigh turned on his side and slugged his pillow, miffed that Margie would take offense over such an inconsequential matter. A disappointing culmination to an otherwise wonderful day.

Richard telephoned one morning in July. “Hi, Kiddo.” He sounded upbeat and rather pleased with himself. “I have the day off today. Would it be permissible for me to take you to lunch? I have something to tell you.”

“Don’t tell me you’ve joined the Navy!”

Richard laughed. “No, nothing like that. Can I pick you up in about an hour?”

“I’ll have to bring along Greggie. If that’s okay, then yeah. But at least give me a hint what it’s about.”

“You know me better than that. I’ll see you in a bit.”

Margie had never been too long on patience and was all but pacing the floor by the time Richard rang the doorbell. She picked up Greggie, placed him on her hip, grabbed the diaper bag, opened the door, brushed past Richard with a smile and a brief “hi,” and headed for his car. If she had to wait until lunch to hear what he had to say, then he’d better make it snappy. She didn’t even bother pulling the house door shut, so Richard obligingly took care of it, chuckling over her restless conduct.

“I don’t know my way around out here,” he acknowledged as he started the car’s engine. “Where’s a good place to eat?”

“Hmm,” pondered Margie. “You want hamburgers or restaurant food?”

“Let’s go somewhere nice,” Richard suggested.

“There’s a place we like in Van Nuys, if you want to go that far.”

Richard chuckled. “Seems to me you’re the only one in a hurry.”

Margie shrugged. “I guess I can wait that long.” She lifted the corners of her mouth as she looked sideways at him. “But it won’t be easy!”

Richard still found himself charmed by his cousin. Ah,

well, she was a married woman, and that was a fact he couldn't ignore. Presently he pulled up in front of the recommended restaurant and escorted Margie inside. They requested a highchair for Greggie and were subsequently seated in a booth.

Richard opened his menu, indicated his preference for a Cobb salad, and asked Margie what she'd like.

"What's a Cobb salad?" she queried. "Is it any good?"

He merely looked at her and lifted an eyebrow.

"I guess that was a stupid question. But what is it?"

"Well, you remember when we went to the Brown Derby to eat?"

"Of course I remember. That was one of the highlights of my life!"

Richard smiled, recalling Margie's unabashed high spirits of that night, then went on to explain. "Well, Bob Cobb, who used to own the Brown Derby, was in his restaurant kitchen one night, looking for a snack. He pulled a bunch of stuff out of the refrigerator and started chopping and, voilà, the Cobb salad was born. It has lettuce, of course, and tomatoes, and bacon, eggs, ham, avocados, and bleu cheese. Hmm, not sure what else. Anyway, Sid Grauman, of Grauman's Chinese Theater, who was with Cobb that night and helped him eat his 'snack,' liked it so well that he asked in the restaurant the next day for a 'Cobb salad.' It was such a hit that it was put on the menu and became an overnight sensation. They say that Jack Warner, of Warner Brothers, used to send his chauffeur over about every day to pick him up a carton of it.

"So, why don't you try one?"

"I think I will. But how do you come by all of these little tidbits of information?" Margie had never ceased to be amazed at her cousin's vast knowledge of trivia.

Richard shrugged. "I just keep my eyes and ears open."

The waitress appeared at that moment, took their order, and returned to the kitchen. Margie could wait no longer for Richard's news. "Okay, now. Spill it!"

"Well, actually, I have two things to tell you. First of all, I think you'll be happy to know that I have quit the 'devil drink.'"

"Really, Richard? Oh, that's wonderful! I could kiss you!" He gave her a look that said, "Oh, yeah?" and she laughed and clarified, "A figure of speech. So how long ago? What made you decide?"

"Well, that's sort of the other thing I have to tell you." Richard raked one hand through his dark hair, wondering over her probable reaction to his tidings. After several seconds, he blurted, "I've met someone."

It took a minute for Margie to process the information. "What do you mean? You're getting married?" She was shocked and not too thrilled about this sudden turn of events, though she had to admit that it was ludicrous, under the circumstances, for her to feel jealous. Richard needed a wife, and it had been her own choice, long ago, to relinquish her chance at that coveted position. She was now getting on with her life, and he needed to do the same. Margie took a breath and adopted a happy expression. "Who is it? Where did you meet?"

"As you may have heard, I've been directing the orchestra for our community theater group."

"Mom mentioned it to me," Margie acknowledged.

"Well, Linda's one of our cellists–she's a very accomplished musician." Margie could manage no more than a nod–this was worse than she thought; the woman was gifted and probably beautiful to boot. Richard continued, "We started talking one night after rehearsal and, as they say, one thing led to another."

"Mmm. So how long have you been dating?" Margie asked, not because she really wanted details, but in an effort to act unaffected by Richard's news. Her cousin, however, was no fool. He'd known her too long and too well to be taken in by her less-than-stellar performance. He sat silent for several moments, waiting for her to quit busying herself with Greggie and look at him. That, however, was the last thing she wanted to do. She knew he could read every nuance of expression that had ever crossed her face. If she so much as glanced in his direction, it would be the end of her pretense. Finally, however, she could endure the silence no longer, and their eyes met.

"I've upset you," Richard noted, apologetic.

"I'm just surprised," Margie equivocated, though she knew he wasn't buying it. "There's no reason for me to be upset. This is what I want for you: to settle down and be happy."

Richard slipped from his side of the booth, crossed over, and slid in next to Margie. Turning sideways to face her, he placed his hand over hers and commanded, "Look at me." Margie lifted tearful eyes to meet his own and felt excruciating pain at the evidence of grief she saw there. He seemed, himself, about to weep. "Margie, my sweet little dimwit, you know I've always loved you. No one can ever mean to me what you do, what you always have and always will. If I'd had my way, we'd be sitting here as husband and wife, not merely as cousins." Margie could contain the tears no longer, and her sobbing induced the destruction of Richard's own reserve.

She threw her arms around his neck and wept quietly and bitterly against his shoulder. "Oh, Richard, I've made such a mess of things, haven't I?"

"Yes," he agreed succinctly.

A choke that might have been a laugh escaped her lips, bringing on more tears. "I love you, too, Richard. I always have, and it's unforgivable for me to say it now–now that I'm married to Leigh. But I've been so stupid, and I'm so very sorry–sorry for you and sorry for me. And now it's too late. I can't do anything to fix it."

Richard placed his hands on either side of Margie's face and gently pulled her away from him. "We all make stupid unfixable mistakes," he acknowledged, stroking her cheek with the back of his fingers. "No one knows that better than I do. Right now, I'd like to beg you to leave Leigh and come away with me to some exotic island on the far side of the world." Margie began to shake her head and Richard went on. "I know. You would never do that. You're exasperatingly loyal. Ah, Margie, what is there for us now but to try to make the best of a bad situation? That's what I'm trying to do, forget the past and get on with my life. Can you understand?"

Margie nodded and grabbed a stack of napkins from the table to dry her sopping face. "So, how soon is the wedding?"

Richard leaned back and folded his arms. "We're thinking about Christmastime."

Margie nodded again, searching her mind for something pleasant and positive to say. "It's nice that she's a musician, too; that gives you a lot in common," was the best she could do.

Afterward, Margie couldn't even remember if they'd eaten their salads. She chided herself for her egoistic reaction to Richard's news, knowing that he was right. They both needed to bridle their love for each other and move forward.

When Leigh returned home from work that night and Margie relayed to him the announcement of Richard's forthcoming marriage, Leigh's response was, "Good for him. I'd say it's about time!" Her husband indicated no suspicion of her distress; at least she had him hoodwinked.

Two days later, Margie answered the telephone to hear Grace on the other end of the line. "Margie, your aunts and I are getting together tomorrow for a sisters' lunch and wondered if you'd like to join us. My treat, of course."

"I'm not exactly one of the sisters."

"No, but you're the only female of the next generation, so we figure you're entitled," Grace noted with a smile in her voice.

"In that case, sure. Where're we going?"

"Tick Tock. We'll pick you up about 11:30."

"I'll be ready." She might have guessed at the restaurant of choice. It had long been a favorite of her mother's.

Margie was excited about her little tête-à-tête with "the girls," but neglected to mention her plans to Leigh; he would no doubt find some reason to object, and she wanted nothing to ruin her buoyant mood. She was still in bright spirits the next day when Grace and her sisters arrived.

"You look like you're feeling well, Dear," Grace observed as they got into the car.

Margie smiled. "Nothing like an afternoon with my three favorite ladies to perk me up." For the duration of the drive, Margie was entertained by the sisters' small talk and gossip and felt like she had stepped back into a former life, one that she couldn't help but miss, now and then.

They arrived at the restaurant, were seated and their orders taken. "Is it all right if I give Greggie a cracker?" asked Leone. With Margie's nod, she proceeded to peel away the cellophane packaging. "He's such a little doll, Margie. Is he always this good?"

"Pretty much. A good thing since I'll soon have my hands full with another one."

"We're glad that you came along today," said Vera. "And that you brought Greggie. Makes us feel young again to have a baby in tow."

"I feel like I'm getting spoiled," Margie remarked. "Richard just took me to lunch a few days ago." At the surprised looks from the other women, she explained, "He wanted to tell me about Linda."

Vera smiled. "She's a lovely girl. I hope they'll be happy."

"Of course they will," Grace assured her. "Now we just need to find someone for you." She raised her eyebrows at her older sister, and Leone nodded an enthusiastic affirmation.

Vera laughed. "I think I'll pass. Once was quite enough."

"You can't judge every man by Lewis," objected Leone.

"She's right," Grace agreed. "We'll just look for someone who's the exact opposite in every way." She began to grin, a twinkle in her eye, as she commenced teasing Vera. "So, first of all, he's got to be a teetotaler, for obvious reasons."

Vera winced. "Don't remind me."

"And tall, since Lewis was short," Leone joined in the game.

"He'll have to have dark hair, since Lewis was light complected."

"With brown eyes."

"And broad shoulders."

Vera laughed. "I think Clark Gable is already taken."

Margie had never met her Uncle Lewis, and photos of him seemed to be nonexistent, so this was all news to her. "He was short and blonde?" she asked. "Who does Richard look like then?"

There was a slight pause in the merriment, as all eyes turned toward Vera, who seemed to be at a loss for words. Then Grace laughed. "Oh, we figure he's a throwback to another generation."

At that point, their food was served, and the subject of Vera's proposed manhunt was dropped.

Chapter XIX

In September, Margie received a disturbing phone call from her mother. "Margie?" she began, an indication of distress in her voice. "Daddy and I just came from the doctor's office." At that point, she broke down and wept.

"Mom?" Margie was terrified; her mother was one of the most self-controlled women she knew. This had to be something horrific.

"It's your father," Grace managed through her tears.

Understandably, the first word that came to Margie's mind was "cancer." She had, of course, known about her father's previous bout with prostate cancer, but the subsequent surgery had, to her knowledge, been successful, and she had dismissed from her thoughts any possibility of a recurrence.

"What?!" she now impatiently demanded.

"His prostate cancer has metastasized. He's going in for surgery on Tuesday, but they're not very optimistic."

"I thought they got it all before! He hasn't even been sick, has he?" Margie couldn't believe what her mother was telling her.

"You know your father. He never complains."

"Did you know he was sick?"

"I knew he hadn't been feeling his best for the last few weeks, but I had no idea how bad it was."

"But surely they can take care of it!" Both the volume and pitch of Margie's voice were increased by her growing agitation.

Grace paused, composing herself as she formed an answer. The doctor had cautioned her against any high expectations, and, though she didn't want to alarm her daughter, she knew that Margie would need time to assimilate the idea of possibly losing her father. "That will depend on how extensive it is," she said. "They won't know for sure until the surgery. I'll call you on Tuesday as soon as I find out anything. Keep your father in your prayers."

Margie had always expected her parents to live to be 100 (or close to it). She had never even contemplated the death of a family member–she knew it would happen eventually but trusted it would be in the distant future–especially her daddy; he was indestructible. His life had been miraculously spared in the past; it could surely happen again.

During the early years of George and Grace's marriage, he had driven a truck for a living. One moonless night, as he was proceeding along a deserted road, he thought he saw a man standing on the pavement in the way of his fast-approaching vehicle. As he slammed on the brakes, all of the faulty bands, whose defects had formerly gone undetected, broke. Fortunately, he was on a slight incline, and the truck rolled slowly to a halt. George firmly set the hand brake and jumped from the cab. He peered into the darkness surrounding him, but there was no sign of a soul and no answer to his shouts. As he proceeded to hike along in the direction he'd been heading, he came to the crest of a steep downward grade. It was apparent that, had he continued driving on, he would have lost control of his rig and probably been killed.

Then, many years later, on a return flight from a business meeting in Washington, D.C., he had decided, on the spur of the moment, to deplane in Colorado and pay his brother a surprise visit. That evening on the news, it was announced that the plane on which he'd been a passenger had gone down in the Grand Canyon. There were no survivors. That particular tragedy caused the whole nation to gasp. The famous movie star Carol Lombard–Clark Gable's favorite leading lady, on screen and off–was one of the fatalities.

Margie prayed fervently for another miracle on his behalf, but this was one prayer that would be answered with a "no."

The funeral was held six weeks later at the church in Westchester and was attended by more than 300 people. George had left his mark on society. Grace, Jack, and Margie stood by the casket greeting family, friends, and coworkers, as they filed past to pay their respects. Grace was bombarded with expressions of gratitude and appreciation from people she'd never before met. George had helped them set up a new business or paid for a lifesaving operation or supported them on a mission for their church or paid off one of their debts–on and on and on.

As Richard approached and embraced Margie, she completely broke down. Wrapping her arms around his waist and laying her head against his chest, she sobbed freely, as he stroked her hair and attempted to console her. "What can I say, Margie? I am so sorry. Uncle George was a good man. He always treated me well. You're a lot like him, you know." Sweeter words couldn't have been spoken. Margie loved her mom but had always wanted to be just like her dear daddy.

Two days after her father was buried, Margie gave birth to a beautiful daughter, whom she and Leigh named Georgeanne. Whereas Greggie, upon entering this world, had cried inconsolably for one night, Georgeanne screamed nonstop for three months.

It soon became evident that Leigh would not lose any sleep because of a colicky baby. He simply placed a pillow over his head and snoozed on, while Margie rocked, patted, paced, rubbed, sang, fed, bounced, and burped. She began to wonder if either of them would survive.

But the exhausting nights, as soon as they were a thing of the not-too-distant past, faded from memory as Georgeanne's rotten disposition began to dissolve into irresistible charm.

The arrival of Richard's wedding invitation erased every other thought from Margie's mind. She was naturally obliged to attend, and truth be told, she wouldn't have missed it for the world; she was too anxious to meet the person who had replaced her.

The marriage was performed at Richard's church, with the reception to follow immediately. Leigh and Margie slipped unobtrusively into the back row just before the ceremony began. She glanced toward the front of the chapel and swallowed hard at the sight of Richard standing there in a tux–she had never before seen him thus donned and would have bet that it would never happen (his bride must be very persuasive); the look of him made her heart melt.

The wedding march began and all eyes turned in anticipation. As Linda appeared through the back doors, Margie's initial assumptions about her appearance were substantiated. She was indeed beautiful: thin as a willow, with long auburn hair, flawless ivory skin, and brown eyes. Statuesque would be an apt description, and Margie's green-eyed monster became her conspicuous companion. She heard little of what was said until the bishop pronounced them man and wife. At that point, Margie's tears began to flow.

"What's wrong?" inquired Leigh.

Margie shook her head. "Don't you know that women always cry at weddings?"

As she and Leigh waited in line to greet the bride and groom, she observed every smile, every gesture of affection, every subtlety of emotion displayed between the couple; her heart was broken, but her smile was fixed. As she approached the wedding bower, Richard's head snapped suddenly in her direction. His smile faded slightly and was quickly replaced with a more rueful substitute. He held out his hands and Margie placed her palms against his, curling her fingers around the familiar grip. She couldn't take her eyes off of his beseeching face. Several seconds passed before Richard recovered his good manners and proceeded with the formalities. "Linda, this is my cousin, Margie, and her husband, Leigh."

Linda's face brightened. "So this is the famous Margie that I've heard so much about!" Margie tried to perceive some hint of guile in her words but found nothing to indicate that she wasn't totally ingenuous. Linda continued, "It's so wonderful to finally meet you. I just know we're going to become very good friends." Margie somehow managed to utter a proper response before moving on wobbly knees to one of the refreshment tables.

"Linda seems nice enough," observed Leigh as they seated themselves.

"Yeah, she seems very nice. Do you think it's for real?"

"Wha'd'ya mean?"

"Well, it's just hard to imagine that anyone is really that full of sweetness and light."

Leigh shrugged. "I can only judge by what I see, and it looks to me like she's just what she seems to be."

Margie hated to admit it, but he was probably right.

Just prior to their wedding, Richard and Linda had purchased a modest residence in Torrance, several miles south of Margie's Encino home, and shortly after the first of the new year, they invited Margie's family for dinner. Margie was still struggling with the actuality of Richard's marital status and had some misgivings about such an evening. Still, she accepted the invitation–her curiosity perhaps getting the better of her judgment. She wanted to observe the dynamics between the newlyweds, hoping for . . . what? A confirmation that Richard was–or possibly wasn't–happy? An indication that Linda was less than the perfect persona she portrayed at the wedding? Some hint that the honeymoon was over? Most likely, all of the above.

Margie felt slightly ill at ease as they were welcomed into her cousins' new home. She was prepared to find fault with everything Linda did, from the meal she'd prepared to the color of paint on her walls, but after spending a short time in Linda's company, Margie found it impossible to hold out against her warm personality. She could even visualize a close friendship developing between the two of them, a realization that left her in shock.

With a little after-dinner coaxing from Margie, Linda was persuaded to bring out her cello and play, with Richard accompanying her on the piano (this gave Margie a twinge and Leigh a headache). Linda's musical skill was to be envied, and Margie's eyes were again definitely green, but the shameful emotion was counterbalanced by the unexpected connection she felt toward the other woman.

Nevertheless, in the coming months, Margie missed Richard's formerly frequent phone calls and occasional visits. His attentions had been diverted–and rightly so, though the knowledge of its rightness didn't begin to compensate for the hollow feeling in Margie's chest.

Chapter XX

When Georgeanne was eight months old, Margie happily discovered that another child was on the way. The production line was now moving along in just the manner she had intended. As thrilled as she was to once again have a bun in the oven, Margie could find nothing pleasant about pregnancy itself, except that she could eat whatever she wanted–not that she didn't gain weight, but that it didn't matter since no one knew how much of it was baby and how much was Margie. Other than that, the grueling nine months were merely something to be not-so-patiently endured. But at the end there was always a giant, yet tiny, reward.

One evening, soon after their second son, David, was born, Leigh announced that he had received a tentative job offer from a man who owned a small architectural firm in Denver. For Margie, this came right out of left field. They had just finished dinner and the two older children were playing with their toys on the living room floor; the baby was sleeping peacefully in his bassinet. Margie had cleared the table and begun washing dishes while Leigh remained in the kitchen, biding his time, not wanting to drop his bombshell until he was reasonably sure that they would have a few moments without interruption. “I didn’t even know you were looking,” she complained, turning from the sink to frown at him.

“I wasn’t, really. This guy was visiting Fred, a friend of mine at work, and they invited me to have lunch with them. He seemed to take a liking to me and, when I told him I had a background in art, he said he might have an opening in his company for someone like me. I could go to school at the same time and get my degree in architecture.”

“Are you sure that’s what you want to do?” Margie wondered if Leigh had what it would take to hold down a job and, at the same time, complete his bachelor’s degree and go on to pursue his master’s. She was also fearful of what the change would do to their tenuous hold on financial stability. Over the last few years, her relationship with Leigh had been improving concurrently with his increases in salary. Not because she loved money–though she certainly didn’t disdain it–but because Leigh was so much happier when they didn’t have to pinch every penny. She wouldn’t be easily persuaded to give up the progress they had made in their marriage.

“I’d finally be working in my field,” Leigh went on. “This is the kind of break I’ve been wishing for! You could get a part-time job to help out with finances.”

Margie’s temper flared. “I already have a full-time job, in case you haven’t noticed.”

“I don’t mean during the day. I could keep an eye on the kids for a few hours at night while I study, and you could go to work.”

Margie merely stared at him. Her own parents had not only struggled through the Depression but had weathered many subsequent hard times as well before George finally began to climb the ladder of success. Yet Margie knew for a fact that George had never so much as suggested that Grace be even partially responsible for putting food on the table. And Richard, he would die before he asked his wife to get a job. Why must Leigh persistently fall short when compared with the other men in her life?

From the bedroom, little Davey's cries offered Margie the excuse she needed to escape before she said something she might later regret. "I've got to go feed the baby," she said. "We'll talk about this later."

They went to bed in silence that night, each mulling over the possibility of a drastic alteration in their lives and each forming a totally different opinion about the advisability of such a change. But, in the end, it was Margie who gave in–at least as far as the move; she still believed that a mother's place was with her children and refused to consider working away from home. They would just have to make do.

As soon as the job offer was a certainty, she sullenly packed up their belongings, helped load them into the small U-Haul, and then cried throughout the seventeen-hour journey to their new location.

Dear Richard and Linda,

We arrived in Denver with bigger bags under our eyes than in the trunk of the car. Leigh drove most of the way while I tried to keep the children happy–not an easy task under the best of circumstances. Then while I drove, Leigh slept, and the children mostly cried. Sure am glad the journey is over–not so sure I'm glad to be where it brought me.

Leigh seems to think he will do really well in this new job and going to school at the same time; we'll see.

The area is nice and the weather is beautiful. We will be moving (tomorrow) into a small (very small) duplex but ha-

ven't been able to sell our California house as yet. We've turned it over to a real estate agency and are hoping for the best. Don't know if we'll make any money on it or not. The fees might eat up all the equity, and we had to borrow the money from Daddy for the down payment in the first place.

Meanwhile, how are you two doing? I'm excited that your family is going to increase by one (I assume it's only one) in the very near future. Congratulations! Our three are keeping me very busy, but I'm loving every minute of it. Only nine more to go!

Time certainly flies, doesn't it? Greggie is two and a half now and thinks he's a big guy. Wants to carry little Davey around the house all the time. Wish he could! Sure would save my back! Linda, are you doing okay with the morning sickness?–that term is really a joke. It's been my experience that it's morning, noon, and nighttime sickness.

Richard, you never thought you were cut out to be a dad, but I guess you're going to have to change your tune now. You're going to love it!

Hope all is well with you.

Love,

Margie

Chapter XXI

Shortly after getting settled, Margie received word that her beloved grandma had suffered a fatal stroke. Margie was heartsick; with all of the preparations for their move, during the past few weeks, she had paid less-than-usual attention to her dear grandmother. How tragic it is, she thought, that we so take for granted the perpetual availability of those we love. Margie had barely allowed enough time to tell her grandma good-bye before they left California. After all that the sweet old lady had meant to her, how could she have been so thoughtless?

Although Margie realized that the price of a flight home would doubtlessly be out of reach, she nonetheless checked with the airlines to determine the cheapest fare, then approached Leigh with the information. He reacted in exactly the way she had anticipated.

"Where are we going to get the money for you to fly to California?" he chided.

"Leigh, it's my grandma's funeral!" Margie pleaded, trying to stay calm.

"Unfortunately, the tickets cost the same, no matter what the occasion, and there's no way we can afford it, unless you've stashed some money away somewhere."

"And how would I ever do that?" Margie's ire was rising.

"Well, then, where's it going to come from?"

"I don't know, Leigh. Why don't you try figuring something out for a change!" Margie stomped into the bedroom and vigorously closed the door behind her. In spite of their nonexistent funds, she had longed for Leigh to tell her that he would somehow make it happen, that he understood how important it was for her to go, and he would do whatever it took to see that she could. Well, no surprises there. He had responded to the problem in typical Leigh-like fashion–roll over and play dead.

Margie accepted the inevitable. She would miss the chance to bid a last good-bye to her dearly cherished grandmother. And she would find it almost impossible to forgive her husband.

On the day of the funeral, Richard telephoned. "Why didn't you tell me you needed help getting here?" he fumed. "I'd have sent you a ticket." How like Richard to not only understand her feelings, but to offer assistance as well.

"You couldn't afford to do that," Margie stated flatly.

"I'd have found a way," came the unhesitating reply.

Margie almost laughed. Hadn't she longed to hear those exact words from Leigh? "Richard, it's not your responsibility to take care of me."

"Well, somebody needs to!" Richard flung back at her hotly. Then, regretting his untimely words, he backed off. "Sorry. I shouldn't have said that. I just worry about you, that's all."

"I know, but I'm okay."

Richard grunted softly. "You're more than just okay, Kiddo. You're a true survivor."

After his first semester of school, Leigh was discouraged.

"I just don't think I can keep this up," he announced to Margie one night after dinner. "There's never enough time to study, and I'm always worn out at work. The thing is, I don't think my boss will keep me on if I'm not going after my degree."

"So what will you do?" she asked, worried.

"Insurance companies are always looking for agents. I think I could do that."

"Can you make enough money at it?" Margie was not incognizant of the fact that most insurance agents worked strictly on commission.

"I guess it depends on how good a salesman I turn out to be," he answered lightly.

"You could have sold insurance in California," Margie muttered testily.

"What?"

She shook her head. "Nothing."

"Never mind. I heard you. How was I to know that things wouldn't turn out the way we expected? Anyway, I know guys who've made a lot of money in insurance, and I think it's worth a try. Our finances might be a little tight at first; it takes awhile to build up a clientele, but you could always get a job to help out until I get established."

"We've had this discussion before, Leigh. I'm not going to work!"

But she did. She had no choice if they were to survive. The new business was, indeed, slow in starting, and then quick in finishing. Leigh was not exactly a self-motivator. For several months, he stayed home with the children while Margie resentfully earned their living–a very meager living at that. The longer she was forced to stay in the workplace, the angrier she became, and the more she regretted the choices she had made, choices that had resulted in an impossible marriage far away from home. Other than her children, the only thing that brought her pleasure was the ongoing correspondence with her cousin.

Dear Richard and Linda,

I was so excited to hear about the arrival of your little cherub, and I love the name you've chosen. Gideon was one of my favorite heroes in the scriptures–strong, courageous, smart, clever, and forceful. Your little guy has some big shoes to fill. But, if he's anything like his dad, it won't be a problem. Who does he look like? Send me some photos! Linda, how are you feeling?

I'm still working, trying to put food on the table and so angry about being forced to do so. I miss my children terribly, especially my little Davey. He is such a wonderful gift. A happier child you couldn't find anywhere. He is walking now, and just flits from one thing to another, so interested in everything–busy, busy, busy. His little eyes fairly sparkle at every new discovery. He's so perfect, it scares me!

Leigh is still trying to find himself, I guess. I wonder if our spirits were put into the wrong bodies. Maybe I should have been the man and he the woman! Except that I love being a woman. They always accuse us (women) of, deep down, wishing we were men, but I think it's the other way around. I think most men secretly envy women. What about you, Richard? Do you wish you were a woman? (Ha ha–I guess not!) You were obviously meant to be a man–a very special one. Linda, I hope you know how lucky you are!

By the way, it's time to start brainwashing that baby–you can't begin too early, you know–so that he'll grow up believing that his cousin Margie is the greatest thing on two legs.

Won't be easy–better start now!
Can't wait to see him!
Love,
Margie

Eventually, circumstances forced Leigh to once again become the family breadwinner. A few months after learning of the birth of Richard's son, Gideon, Margie again found herself pregnant. Leigh was noncommittal in his response to the news of another offspring, and Margie had mixed feelings about bringing an additional child into their unstable home. Initially, she had thought that another baby might help to heal the abrasions in her marriage. She still hoped, perhaps against hope, for that particular miracle but was becoming more and more resigned to the fact that there was probably no Band-Aid big enough. This, however, was not the only thing that was troubling her. She had recently begun having strong impressions about the direction that their future should take and was nervous about discussing her feelings with Leigh.

One evening, after the children were in bed, she approached her husband, with much trepidation over what she had to tell him. He was settled in front of the television set, engrossed in an old war movie. "Leigh, I need to talk to you."

"Wait just a second, Hon. This is an important part."

Margie sighed in submission. She knew she wouldn't have his attention until the movie was over. "I'll talk to you later then. I think I'll go to bed and read for awhile."

There was no response, and it was questionable whether her words had even registered. No matter; she'd broach the subject when he finally retired for the night.

After putting on her nightgown and grabbing her current read from the dresser in their crowded bedroom, she climbed under the covers and flipped open the pages. But she was too apprehensive to concentrate, so she lay staring at the ceiling, mentally reviewing her little speech.

Finally, she heard the TV go silent, and soon Leigh entered the room and sat on the edge of the bed to undress. "Leigh, can we talk now?" she began.

"I'm pretty tired. Can it wait until morning?"

"I don't think so," Margie stated vehemently. "I need to tell you something and if I don't tell you now, I won't be able to sleep."

This caught Leigh's attention, and he twisted his body sideways to face her. "Okay. Shoot."

"First of all, do you believe that God sometimes tells us things in our dreams?"

Leigh shrugged. "I dunno. I've never really thought about it. Why?"

"Because for several nights now, I've had a recurring dream about us moving. I think we need to leave Denver."

"Are you nuts? I just started a new job!" He smirked as he returned to the business of undressing. "You've been eating too much pizza before bed."

Leigh thought he was being funny, only Margie didn't laugh. "I was afraid you'd say something like that. But I really believe it's what we're supposed to do. So the question is: Are you with me or not?"

Leigh stopped to stare at her. "Are you saying you'd go without me?" He was taken aback.

Margie sighed heavily. "No, of course not. But I feel strongly about this, and I want you to trust me."

"Where is it you think we're supposed to go?" Leigh asked as he slipped on his pajamas, still giving the idea little credence.

"I'm not sure yet. I'm still trying to figure that out."

"Well, when you do, let me know. Meanwhile, I've got to get some sleep. Seven a.m. comes early." He climbed into bed and turned on his side, facing away from her.

Margie was frustrated–though not surprised–at Leigh's response, but she had at least planted the idea in his mind. She knew him well enough to realize that, if she gently prodded him now and then, eventually he would submit to whatever she was determined to do. On the other hand, if Leigh wished for something that Margie objected to, all she had to do was . . . nothing. Without her encouragement and slight nagging, nothing was ever accomplished. She was definitely the leading force in their marriage and not overly pleased about it.

Settling on a destination was her next major priority, but in the end, the decision was made for her. Margie had sent Leigh's résumé to several mountain west and Pacific coast companies who were advertising in the help wanted section of the local newspaper. Leigh was quickly rewarded with an interview and subsequent job offer from an advertising agency in Salt Lake City. He was unexpectedly excited about his new place of employment; with any luck, he might possibly find his niche at last.

The prospect of another move, especially during the first months of her pregnancy when she was feeling so ill, filled Margie with dread. If she hadn't felt compelled to follow her impressions, she would have called the whole thing off. Fortunately, their belongings were minimal, so a rented U-Haul trailer–in the smallest size available–accommodated everything they needed to transport.

After spending a week in a Salt Lake City motel while they searched for a place to live, they finally located a small two-bedroom apartment in which they could immediately set up housekeeping. It was extremely crowded, but it wasn't the first time they had been jammed into tight quarters.

Greggie was a very active four-year-old by this time while Georgeanne, who was not quite three, preferred the quiet company of her dolls. Davey, at a year and a half, had never bothered walking; as soon as he had his balance, he began to run-everywhere. Margie had a difficult time keeping him out of harm's way. His exuberant spirit never seemed satisfied. There was a brightness and joy about him that immediately won over even the most reserved hearts. No one could resist that little tow-headed child, least of all Margie. He and she both knew that he had her securely hooked and reeled in.

Because of their cramped living conditions, Margie and the children often walked to the park, which was just two blocks away. It was a delight to watch her little ones play on the endless expanse of lawn, with Greggie running back and forth between swing and slide, and Davey, on his little stubby legs, tirelessly scurrying after his big brother. Even Georgeanne seemed to enjoy the wide-open space, though she was too frightened to join the boys on the playground.

Margie always packed a lunch to take along, with half a peanut butter sandwich for each child and usually an orange or an apple for them to share. Greggie was hard put to be satisfied with the meager fare and, on one of their outings, complained apologetically, "I'm still hungry, Mama." Margie's heart turned upside down. She wanted so much for her children, and the fact that they might occasionally be hungry tore her apart.

Then she noticed that Davey's soft pudgy fist, holding his sandwich with three small bites taken out, was thrust toward Greggie. "Here, Geggie," he offered with an ear-to-ear smile. It was all Margie could do to hold back the tears as the older boy looked at her to see if it was permissible.

"How about if I divide it so you can share?" she proposed with a catch in her voice. The simple solution made both of her sweet boys happy. She smiled at them, lifting her eyebrows and widening her eyes in an attempt to staunch the flood that was threatening, but she could not hold it back. Davey's face suddenly clouded as he placed one hand on her cheek, peering deeply into her eyes. "'S'okay, Mommy," he soothed. Margie threw her arms around her tiny child, thinking to herself that she didn't deserve this precious blessing named Davey.

In spite of their less-than-adequate surroundings, Margie was overjoyed to be at home, once again, with her babies, and Leigh, wonder of wonders, was loving his new job. He even started attending church with the family, an activity he had never in his life considered a top priority. Margie was becoming hopeful about the future. Maybe she could make this marriage work after all.

One Sunday morning in November, Margie was, as usual, making a last-ditch effort to locate the children's shoes and socks, which always magically disappeared just before church time. Finally unearthing the last stray, she began to twist it onto Greggie's unwieldy foot.

"Go ahead and carry Davey out to the car," she called to Leigh. "I'll put his shoes on him on the way."

Leigh picked up their youngest, grabbed Georgeanne by the hand, and headed out the door. Margie was tying Greggie's laces when she heard a strange thud outside accompanied by a distressed grunt.

Margie ran to the front door and beheld Leigh lifting himself from the ice-covered driveway, a look of disbelief and torment on his face, and Davey lying on the ground, eyes closed, arms stiff, head arched back, and motionless. Margie uttered a low cry as she rushed to her baby and knelt down, moving her eyes over his body. No blood, she observed. That's good. "Davey?" He was unresponsive. She knew better than to move him, although to leave him on the cold ground seemed an unacceptable alternative. "Call an ambulance!" she ordered, her eyes still on the unconscious child, "and bring me a blanket." She wanted to succumb to the hysteria that threatened to overcome her but would not allow that to happen. Someone had to maintain enough presence of mind to get Davey the help that he needed. Leigh, though himself uninjured, seemed paralyzed by shock. "Leigh!" demanded Margie, turning to face him. "We've got to get him to the hospital! Right now!"

Leigh shook himself out of his stupor and obediently ran into the house to place the phone call and grab a blanket.

As they waited, Leigh managed to explain to Margie what had happened. In his haste to get the children into the car so they wouldn't be late for church, he had not watched his step as he came down off of the porch. His feet had slipped out from under him, and the child had catapulted from his arms. It was obvious, at that point, that Davey must have landed heavily on his head. Margie listened to the account in silence, not trusting herself to speak. She was too angry to offer sympathy, even though she knew that Leigh was in anguish.

Sirens blared as the ambulance approached. Davey's head and neck were first stabilized, then experienced hands lifted him into the back of the emergency vehicle. Margie quickly climbed in beside him, the rear doors were closed and the driver hurried them toward Primary Children's Hospital high up on the Avenues in Salt Lake, with Leigh and the other children following in the car.

Once there, a routine check of Davey's vital signs was performed and an EEG ordered. The results were not encouraging. Davey was admitted, and Margie watched as he was settled into a private room, with wires and tubes anchored and inserted everywhere on his small body. She then returned to the waiting area to apprise Leigh of what little she knew. She found him sitting sullenly, staring at the floor, with the two older children on his lap. He looked up apprehensively as Margie seated herself in the chair next to him. "What did the doctor say?" he asked. "Is Davey going to be all right?"

"I don't know, Leigh. I think we just have to wait and see."

"Margie, I'm so sorry." Leigh's voice gave way and he began to sob. "It just happened so fast!"

Margie nodded. "It's not your fault, Leigh," she stated, although she desperately wanted to blame someone, and Leigh was the logical choice. Had he just been more diligent in keeping the walkways and driveway cleared of snow and ice, this could have been avoided altogether. If anyone were to blame, she knew exactly who that person was. The fact that he was suffering bore no sway with Margie; she was too grief stricken to care.

"Mommy?" Margie heard Greggie's small voice and suddenly realized that he must be terrified by the strange events of the last little while. "Davey's going to get better, isn't he?"

Margie tried to smile at her little son who was attempting so gallantly to put on a brave front. "We all need to pray really hard that he will. Can you do that?" Greggie nodded as she held out her arms to him. He slid down from Leigh's grasp and Margie pulled him close, nuzzling his tousled hair and breathing in his little boy smell. Georgeanne, sensing her mother's distress, also left her father's knee and insisted on climbing into Margie's lap in an effort to give and receive solace. Margie cuddled her children, drawing comfort from their warm softness.

"I'm going to stay here tonight," she told Leigh, "so why don't you take the children home? I'll call you in the morning. Maybe Davey will be awake by then, and we'll have a better idea about what's going on."

But Davey was not awake the next morning, nor the next. On the third day, the doctor, with a grim face, took Margie aside to explain to her the most likely future scenario. "I apologize for having to be blunt with you, Mrs. Monroe, but I don't want you to get your hopes up. The truth is that with injuries of this nature, the prognosis is very poor. In all probability, your son will never regain consciousness. His pupils are fixed and dilated, he's not breathing on his own, and there is absolutely no posturing." Margie blinked in puzzlement. "Sorry," the doctor continued, "that means that when we introduce painful stimuli, there is no response whatsoever. Treatment, in this case, is beyond the scope of our knowledge and abilities." The doctor was obviously distressed. "I can't tell you how sorry I am," he said.

Margie refused to be crushed. She would continue to hope and pray. There was always a chance until there was no chance. The days and weeks dragged by with no signs of improvement while Margie endeavored to juggle her responsibilities at home with her need to be at Davey's side. Without the help of friends and neighbors, it wouldn't have been possible. Even with their help, it was the worst nightmare imaginable.

Greggie and Georgeanne, regardless of the love they felt for their little brother, found it difficult to understand their mother's frequent absences and her distraction even when present. It was frustrating for Margie that she couldn't spread herself thin enough to satisfy the needs of all of her children.

"Mama." Greggie had crept into his parents' bedroom one night as Margie fell wearily into bed.

She turned toward the small voice. "What are you doing awake?" she asked with a touch of annoyance.

"I been thinking about Davey."

Margie pulled back the covers and moved toward the center of the bed, motioning for Greggie to crawl in beside her, then pulled the blanket over him and cradled his head against her shoulder. "I been praying every night," he went on. "Why won't Heavenly Father make him better?"

Margie, herself, would like the answer to that one; what was she supposed to tell Greggie? "I don't know," she finally admitted. "There are lots of things we don't understand about why people get sick and sometimes don't get better, even when we pray for them. But we have to think about what's best for Davey. We may not know what that is, but Heavenly Father does, and He'll do whatever's right. If Davey does . . . leave us, he'll go to a beautiful place where he'll be happy–not sick anymore–and someday, a long time from now, we'll get to see him again."

"Will he come back?"

"No, Sweetheart, but we'll get to go where he is." Greggie seemed satisfied with her explanation; Margie, however, though she knew she had spoken the truth, was not that easily reconciled. She simply wanted Davey back–the real Davey.

Eventually, it was determined that Davey, still comatose, would need to be transferred to a long-term care facility. Margie was heartsick over the move; it was obvious that everyone had given up on him. Now, they would merely keep him comfortable.

For the next two months, Margie lived with total physical and emotional exhaustion and, ultimately, with untold guilt for wishing that this ordeal would soon come to an end, one way or another. Then, when it finally did, she wasn't ready.

Dear Richard,

The one thing I thought I could never endure has happened. Although Davey's sweet, exuberant little spirit has been missing from us for some time, I continued to hold out the hope that he would one day awake and return to us. But instead, he has left us for good. I can hardly say the words. Why am I still here? For that matter, why is everyone I see going on about their business just as if nothing out of the ordinary has occurred? Don't they know that one of heaven's brightest lights has been extinguished? I can't bear this! Tell me why a child with so much love to offer should be deprived of all future opportunities to do so. Am I being punished for something? The Lord knows I was never worthy of him, but why then was he given to me in the first place? Just so I could suffer when he was taken away? Oh, I know–I'm talking nonsense. But it's just so hard. I never imagined that something like this could ever happen to me. This is unbearable! I don't know how to live without Davey.

Love,
Margie

My dear Margie,

I received your letter this morning, and it's killing me that I'm not close enough to offer any kind of support. You are a great woman–don't ever think that you weren't worthy of Davey. And no, you're not being punished! That's the grief talking. You know that the Lord doesn't punish us in that way. What He has done is bless you with a child who was too good to stay on this earth. Think how much He must love you to place in you that kind of trust. As for Davey, the love you have given him, he'll never forget, and when you meet him again on the other side, you'll see one happy man run to greet you. You have shown great strength in dealing with the events of the last few months, and I know that the Lord is pleased with you. It's obvious from what you've told me that Davey was a valiant spirit. I wish I could have known him.

You have my love and concern,

Richard

Chapter XXII

During the chaos of the last few weeks, Margie had tried to ignore her ever-enlarging belly. At the present moment, she even resented the fact that she was again pregnant. No one could ever replace Davey, yet that's what it felt like she was trying to do. The thought revolted her. Nevertheless, much as she would like to, this was one project that couldn't be postponed nor cancelled and, in February, baby Cadence arrived, and Margie was once again caught up in the taxing routine of infant care.

Leigh was thankfully doing well at his job, and he and Margie felt that the time was propitious for finding a permanent residence with room enough for the family to grow. They settled on a modest but comfortable home in Bountiful, which, in comparison with past abodes, seemed to Margie like a mansion.

Though Davey's bittersweet memory was never far from her thoughts, life was good again. Leigh seemed happier than he had been since the day of their "I dos"; Margie was staying at home, where she wanted to be, caring for her family, and the children appeared to be thriving, emotionally as well as physically.

So why could she not rid herself of this incessant feeling of discontent? No matter how much she accomplished–and her friends were forever amazed at what she could achieve in any given period of time–it was never enough to fill the void. On an evening when this riddle was weighing extra heavily on her mind, she lay in bed, too restless to sleep, willing herself to be satisfied with the status quo. Finally, giving up all hope of slumber, she rose and crept outside to the front porch. There she sat on the top step and leaned her body sideways against the railing. The night was clear, with a cool breeze blowing from the east, rustling the leaves on the lone cottonwood tree in the middle of the front lawn. Margie huddled into herself. She was reminded of a song, popular a few years back–on second thought, more years back than just a few–and began to hum, the lyrics singing themselves in her mind. It had a haunting melody and spoke of trembling trees, an evening breeze, and the seashore, where two hearts met. The words released in Margie an avalanche of tender memories from long ago.

Margie gazed up at the stars, which were out in all of their glory. She was gratified when she recognized the Big Dipper and Orion. Her cousin had taught her well, it seemed. Slowly, an unexpected tear trickled down her cheek as she longingly recalled her introduction to the galaxies and the young Richard who had so gently instructed her. "Oh, Richard," she murmured, "how I miss you. How I wish . . ." but she wouldn't allow her thoughts to take her any further down that path. She wiped her face with her fingers and silently vowed that she would accept her life–just the way it was–and, with the Lord's help, make the best she could of it.

The next couple of years scurried by and, suddenly, it was time for Georgeanne to begin kindergarten. Greggie had begun school the year before, so protocol was old hat for Margie. But Georgeanne seemed less advanced than Greggie had at that age, and this caused Margie some concern about her beautiful little daughter's mental capabilities. For the past two or three years, she had managed to suppress her suspicions, but they were painfully resurrected at the first conference with Georgeanne's kindergarten teacher, when the school counselor–contrary to normal procedure–asked to be included in the interview.

"I've noticed some slight aberrations in Georgeanne's learning patterns," he announced. "I'm not sure that it's anything to be overly anxious about, but it might be a good idea to have a mental workup done, possibly a brain scan, just to see. You can take her to the state health department in Salt Lake, and it won't cost you anything."

Obediently, Margie made an appointment for the following week and took Georgeanne for an evaluation. The opinion of the doctor on staff was that the little girl was slightly diminished mentally but should be able to lead a fairly normal life. Margie left the office feeling optimistic.

But, as time progressed, it became evident that Georgeanne's impairment was more than minimal. The older she got, the more profound her disability became.

This was a grave disappointment and a heavy burden for Margie, combined with the fact that no more babies had come nor pregnancies begun for the past two and a half years. Margie's plan for a houseful of healthy, happy children was far from materializing. But then, Margie's plan for her life had not worked out either. Although she had always been superficially aware that everyone had their problems, she had facetiously predicted mostly fair skies and pleasant days for her own future. Needless to say, fate had intervened with her own ideas.

Chapter XXIII

As the children became older and more responsible, Leigh began to better enjoy their companionship. He planned excursions to the museums in town and visits to art exhibits at Brigham Young University in Provo, as well as other more commonplace outings. Margie was pleased that he seemed to be building a relationship with his youngsters–two of them; he believed it would be a waste of time and money to take Georgeanne along ("She wouldn't understand what she was seeing anyway"). Margie stayed home with her older daughter on these occasions, grateful that at least Gregg and Cadence were learning to know their father–it would be beneficial for both generations.

Cadence was growing into everything her mother had hoped for in a daughter. She was bright, cheerful, obedient, and cooperative, and she loved music. Gregg had also shown, at an early age, a proclivity for music, but due to the limited finances of the Monroe family, had not, as yet, received any formal training. Margie had fretted over this for many years and, by the time Gregg was a happy twelve-year-old, had decided that piano lessons would now become a priority, not only for Gregg, but also for Cadence. Leigh's job was stable–

he had even received a promotion and several wage increases during the past eight years–so Margie felt justified in the added expense. Georgeanne, she realized, would never have the capability to pursue serious study, even though she had a sweet voice and often could be heard singing as she played with her Barbie dolls.

An old upright piano was purchased and immediately Cadence began picking out melodies, even before a teacher was found. Margie could have taught her own children had she ever acquired the patience for such an endeavor, but she knew her limitations and thought it best to leave their musical education in someone else's hands.

Gregg enjoyed the piano and showed great talent for it, but he also played football on a junior city league, and when his buddies discovered that he was participating in "sissy stuff," his artistic pursuits were quickly abandoned. Margie, herself, was now singing in a trio with two friends from church, performing at parties, store openings, and conventions, as well as church meetings and family reunions. At this point, her life was so fulfilling that it frightened her. She was expecting the "other shoe to drop" momentarily.

Dear Margie,

Thought I should let you know that we've had a change of address. We're now living in Canoga Park, out near your old stomping grounds. Got tired of the "big city" traffic! Of course, things around here are growing so fast, it probably won't be long before we're back in the city again–without even moving! Mom has sold her house in Westchester and is living with us until she can decide where she wants to settle. I have to say Linda is a good sport about her live-in mother-in-law. As you know, Mom isn't the easiest person to have around. And, with age, her idiosyncrasies only become more pronounced. I manage to stay out of reach for much of the time, so that means Linda gets the brunt of it.

Sounds like you're having fun with your trio. I'd like to hear you, but I don't see that happening anytime soon. Happy to hear that Leigh's job is working out and you're able to do some of the things you've always wanted to, such as music lessons for the kids. Be glad that they're playing a normal instrument. Gideon informed me the other day that he wants to take up the bagpipes! You gotta wonder about a kid who longs to play the vacuum cleaner!

As always, I'm here if you need me. Keep me in your happy thoughts.

Love,

Richard

Chapter XIX

Margie's anxiety over the future proved to be well founded, though she never could have imagined how devastating a disaster it would be. With the advent of Gregg's seventeenth birthday, his formerly even-tempered behavior became more and more erratic. This young man who had always been so easygoing and obedient suddenly had bursts of unwarranted intense anger, alternating with lengthy periods of lethargy, and Margie had no idea what could possibly be causing the startling change in his personality. He also quit going to church and began hanging around with some of what Margie termed the "low life" at his high school.

She might have dismissed it as a normal teenage phase–Gregg was, after all, her oldest and therefore her first close encounter with seventeen-year-old male hormones, at least from a parent's perspective–except that his whole persona changed. He bore no resemblance to the vigorous, lighthearted boy he had once been.

Her eventual education in the matter was garnered one evening at a session of her book club, as her friends unwittingly began to discuss the symptoms of drug abuse; they didn't have an inkling that Margie was experiencing firsthand exposure. Their interest had not been piqued by personal concerns; none of their children had succumbed to its questionable appeal. But they were stricken by the sudden prevalence of addiction among high school students across the nation, and each was anxious to demonstrate her own awareness of the problem–no one wanted to be accused of having her head in the sand when it came to the ills of the modern world. Margie was, of course, cognizant of the fact of drug abuse; she had, however, never become informed about its symptoms, assuming that she would never personally be confronted with the problem. But as she listened to the enlightening conversation that evening, suddenly everything clicked into place.

She was beside herself as she confronted Gregg with her newfound knowledge. "Gregg, we need to talk," she dictated later that evening after cornering him in his bedroom.

"I'm kinda busy right now," he said, not bothering to look up from the magazine he was reading.

"Well, I'm sorry, but this is important."

Gregg rolled his eyes and heaved a sigh, closing his reading material and slapping it down on the bed covers beside him.

"What's going on with you, Gregg?"

"Wha'd'ya mean?" he asked belligerently, still not looking at her.

Collecting all of her courage, she demanded, "Are you smoking marijuana?"

Gregg huffed, twisting his head to one side.

"Don't you understand that that stuff will destroy your brain?" Margie knew that he was proud of his keen intellect and hoped that the fear of losing it might jolt him into reality. But Gregg remained silent, sitting on the bed with arms folded, staring at the ceiling, pretending to be deaf and blind.

"Don't you have any aspirations in life other than going to parties and getting stoned?" Margie threw up her hands in frustration. "What about a wife and family? That used to be important to you. Is it still?"

Gregg finally acknowledged his mother's presence with a begrudged, "Yeah."

"Then, what are you doing?" Margie was screaming at this point, her voice reverberating throughout the house, the rest of her family stunned by the clamor. "Come to your senses, Gregg. You've got to make some major changes, or your life is going to go straight down the tube!"

Gregg merely shrugged and stared at the wall away from his mother. Margie shook her head in futility, turned and left the room, stomped down the stairs to her own bedroom, slammed the door, and flung herself onto the bed, weeping. "Why doesn't he just take a gun to my head?" she wailed to the empty room. "It wouldn't hurt as much."

Gregg's conduct only worsened; it wasn't long before he was using not only marijuana but whatever else he could procure. By the time he graduated from high school, he had completely dissociated himself from the family, coming home only to sleep at night and very little of that. Though he was somehow able to continue working, in spite of his continual lassitude, Margie doubted that his paycheck covered his accelerating habit. But she didn't question the source of his apparent affluence; she didn't want to know.

Leigh's feelings about the situation were nebulous. Margie couldn't decide whether he was afraid to confront Gregg, for whatever reason, or just didn't care. Either way, he kept himself aloof from any involvement, somehow finding it possible to ignore the drama unfolding around him.

Margie, on the other hand, could never escape it and resented Leigh for distancing himself, thus forcing her to deal with it alone, as usual. The sheer unrelenting agony of it tore her apart until she began to harbor thoughts of terminating her life. Had she not understood that death could not put an end to her misery, she might have done more than simply consider it. But even on the other side of the veil, she knew that her spirit would continue to be aware. There was nothing within her power that would allow her to evade the knowledge of her son's rapid decline into degradation.

In lieu of physical death, she chose emotional death, withdrawing from the world around her, refusing to answer the door and the telephone, not speaking to anyone but her immediate family, and then only when absolutely necessary, and avoiding Gregg altogether. Even her letters to Richard ceased.

Soon after Gregg's nineteenth birthday (which, incidentally, he didn't bother to come home for, in spite of the fact that Cadence and Georgeanne had baked his favorite cake and prepared an evening of celebration), he announced that he had found an apartment and was moving out. Margie was ashamed to admit the level of relief she felt. The awareness of his lifestyle would continue to be a weight upon her shoulders but at least she wouldn't have to observe it firsthand.

Nonetheless, she thought her heart would rip apart as she watched her firstborn drive away from the house, his car laden with his every possession. Her torment was not because he was giving up his home, but because he was giving up his soul, and because, in spite of it all, he was still her little boy, her baby. It occurred to her at that moment that there was more than one way to lose a child–death being the easier to bear.

Margie's languor came to an abrupt halt three months later upon hearing from Grace that Richard was in the hospital following a minor heart attack.

"Is he all right?" Her heart was beating so loudly she wondered if she, herself, would end up in ICU.

"Yes. It wasn't serious and hopefully will just serve as a warning to take better care of himself." There was a slight pause as Grace shifted mental gears. "How are you doing? You haven't written for awhile."

"I know. I'm sorry, Mom. Just been busy." It had never been Margie's habit to confide her innermost sorrows to her mother. She chose to let Grace believe that she led a tranquil life. Perhaps it was pride, an attempt to give the impression that she had always made the right choices and done the wise thing, consequently reaping a life of happiness. What a joke!

Richard was soon discharged from the hospital and on the way to recovery. And Margie was gradually, grudgingly, learning to deal with all of the disappointments that had been heaped upon her.

Dear Richard,

I'm glad to know that you're back home again and feeling better. You gave me quite a fright.

Sorry I haven't written for so long. Truth is, I haven't felt like talking to anyone, not even you (hard to believe, huh?). Why didn't anyone ever tell me how difficult life would be? Maybe if I had known what to expect, I wouldn't feel so battered by its realities. When I think of my silly high school dreams and expectations, I wonder whatever made me believe that they could really come true. Too many romantic novels, I suppose (should have stuck with Nancy Drew). The trouble is, I accepted their fantasies as truth.

Why weren't my parents kind enough to warn me, so that I didn't have to discover for myself that the happy, perfect exis-

tence which I so blindly pursued was an impossible fairy tale? Did they simply forget what their own struggles were like? Did they not have any struggles? Or was everyone of their generation a part of some sort of conspiracy? "Don't tell the children about life–they might not be willing to go through with it!"

I am truly devastated by the turn of events within my family. I somehow expected more and better from them (and myself). I know that it's really unforgivable for me to lay my problems on you, especially when you have a pretty heavy load of your own right now. But you're the only one to whom I can bare my soul without fear of rebuttal. Leigh would dismiss my anguish as trivial. Mom would preach to me about "looking on the bright side" and "counting my blessings." But you, dear cousin, simply listen and console. Thank you for that! And thank you for letting me cry on your shoulder–even if you didn't have a choice! I do yearn for one of our long ago heart-to-hearts! At any rate, I will now try to face the day with–not optimism (a sure precursor for disappointment), but perhaps–equanimity.

Love,
Margie

Chapter XXV

In Margie's Sunday school class, the first week in April, the lesson was on the importance of writing personal histories. It wasn't the first time she had heard the admonition, but for some reason this time it struck a chord and she vowed to begin hers. Not only that, she would nag at her mother until she did the same. George, though he always dreamed of writing a book, preferably a bone-chilling whodunit, had never put the events of his own life down in black and white. Now that he was gone, Margie regretted that she hadn't forced the issue while there had still been time. There was so much about her father that she longed to know–and now it was too late to find out. Grace, however, complied with Margie's request and, before too many weeks had passed, mailed her the completed manuscript.

Margie was anxious to examine what her mother had written. Grace had a certain talent for expressing herself, and Margie knew that her biography would make good reading. On an unusually warm evening in May, she carried the handwritten pages to the front porch where she curled up in the lounge chair and embarked on the adventure. Leigh was going to be late getting home, and the girls were occupied in their room, so she'd have a couple of hours to read in peace.

Grace told of growing up during the early 1900s and of her family's struggles with agrarian life. She aptly described a scenario of physical hardship through which was woven a continual thread of familial happiness. That is, until Vera, shortly after her marriage, suffered a tubal pregnancy, which ruptured, necessitating the removal of both fallopian tubes, thus rendering her incapable of bearing children of her own. The whole family was devastated.

Margie jolted and read the passage again. "But," she whispered to herself, "that's impossible. She had Richard." After weighing the cost of a long distance phone call against her nagging curiosity, Margie hurried to the telephone and dialed Grace's number. "Mom? I don't understand."

"Hello, Dear. Nice to hear your voice, too."

"Um, sorry. It really is nice to talk to you. But I've been reading your history, and there's something I don't get. You say that Aunt Vera couldn't have children. What about Richard?"

There was a slight pause at the other end of the line. Then, "Oh, they adopted him."

"Richard's adopted?" Margie couldn't believe what she was hearing. "Mom! Why didn't you tell me this years ago?"

"Well, because Richard has never been told."

"Why not?" demanded Margie.

"You have to understand that things were different than they are now. It was thought that children were better off not knowing."

"But that's stupid!" she ranted.

"Calm down, Margie. How do you know it's stupid? Because some modern psychologist says so?" Grace felt her own irritation rising and immediately brought it under control.

"Well, maybe you're right," she said in a softer tone, "but regardless, that's just the way it was."

Margie felt as if she would explode from pure rage. She wanted to scream and break things, to tear something apart with her bare hands. She picked up the phone base and paced back and forth as far as the cord would allow, trying to harness her emotions.

"Margie? Are you there?" Grace's voice held a note of apprehension.

Margie sat down and took a deep breath. "So why are you telling me now?" she asked.

Grace sighed. "I wanted to tell you years ago, but I couldn't betray Vera's confidence."

"So, I repeat . . . why now?"

"I'm not sure. I guess I'm feeling guilty about keeping it from you. It's been hard, especially knowing how you and Richard felt about each other."

"You knew about that?"

"I guessed. But maybe things have turned out for the best. You both seem to be happy enough with things as they are."

Margie was stunned. "I've got to hang up now, Mom," she said, not unkindly. "I'll talk to you later."

"Margie?" But the line was already dead.

Margie slammed the phone down on the countertop and marched into the living room, picking up a throw pillow and pitching it against the wall as her footsteps retraced themselves from one side of the room to the other. How had they all managed–for surely every adult in the family was in on their hateful little secret–to keep it all hush-hush for so many years? And how different would her own life have been if they had only revealed to her the truth? She pushed her hands into her hair, grasped the locks with her fists, and tugged, wishing to divert the pain from her heart.

Could she ever forgive the duplicity of the three sisters? That's where the whole malicious scheme had originated. She couldn't really fault her daddy and Uncle Ted for respecting their wives' edict. Then another–more disturbing–thought suddenly struck her: Grandma! She had known everything–all of the desires of Margie's heart–and had still kept quiet about the one thing that would have mattered. Even her beloved grandma had deceived her!

Margie retrieved the tossed pillow from the floor and buried her face in it, then screamed with all the force she could muster but still felt no relief. There was nothing to be done at this point. She remembered Richard telling her, years ago, "Things are what they are." He had somehow been able to accept what life had thrown at him and still go on. Could she? Did she have any choice? Returning to the kitchen, she yanked a Kleenex from the box on the counter and mopped up her wet cheeks. She'd have to pull herself together before Leigh came home.

Margie filled a saucepan with water and put some spaghetti noodles on to boil, then placed a half-pound of hamburger in a frying pan and pulled out an onion to chop (at least she'd have an excuse for her red eyes).

The back door opened, and Leigh stepped from the porch into the kitchen. "What's for dinner?" he asked. Margie gritted her teeth. Of all of his irritating habits, this one ranked high on the list.

Ordinarily, she would have squelched any spontaneous response and answered his question without revealing her annoyance, but on this particular night, she was in no mood to dissemble. "Well, if you can possibly drum up enough fortitude to wait for five minutes, you'll find out, won't you!"

Leigh blinked. "What's eating you?"

"Nothing! I just wonder why you always have to ask, 'What's for dinner?' What difference does it make? Your asking isn't going to change what I've fixed. You can either open your eyes and see what's on the stove or wait until I put it on the table, when the big mystery will finally be solved."

Leigh shrugged. "Let me know when you're in a better mood." He then moved into the living room, where he sat down and flipped on the television.

"Well, that was predictable," Margie sighed, as she resumed the business of meal preparation. "Just walk away; that's how we solve all of our problems."

When dinner was ready, she asked Leigh to call the girls. "I'm not very hungry tonight," she told him. "I'll clean up later." She picked up the book she was currently reading and climbed onto her bed. The words on the page blurred before her scratchy pupils. Rubbing her fingers across her eyelids, she tried to clear her vision and force herself to concentrate. She'd simply pretend that this whole thing had never happened, that she'd never learned the truth, and life would eventually return to almost bearable.

Chapter XXVI

Leigh startled Margie one evening by suggesting a vacation trip to California. Some of his high school buddies were putting together a small reunion, about which he had received notification.

"Really?" Margie was ecstatic. She hadn't realized how homesick she was, not only for her family, but just for the California ambience. "How soon?"

"It's in a couple of weeks. I've got some vacation time coming, so I think I can swing it at work." Leigh had, from the beginning, been allowed a week of time off each year from his job, but they had never before taken a trip. Finances, though vastly improved, were still not superfluous, and there was always work enough around the house to keep them homebound.

"Will we be able to visit the family? I'd like to at least see Mom and Jack and Richard and Linda."

"Sure!" Leigh was being extremely accommodating, and Margie was grateful.

The activities of the next two weeks made for high spirits as Margie got the family ready for their upcoming journey. The girls were equally excited at the idea of a "real vacation" and happily assisted with the preparations. Finally, the day arrived; the car was loaded and the family was on board. Gregg had been invited to join them but had chosen not to accept–no great surprise. Margie was determined not to think about her errant son for the next week. This was going to be the hiatus that she had needed for a long time.

As they traversed the hot Nevada desert, Margie reveled in the change of scenery, saguaros and sagebrush instead of green lawns and cottonwood trees. As they crossed into California, she gratefully breathed in the unquestionable aroma of the oleanders that lined the highway. She was home again!

They pulled up in front of Grace's house, and Margie opened the familiar front door. "Mom? We're here!"

Grace emerged from the direction of the kitchen. "I didn't hear you drive up!" She hugged each of the family in turn. "You can put your things in your old room. The girls can sleep in Jack's room. Dinner's just about ready, so get washed up."

Conversation around the table that evening was a bit stilted, and Margie remembered that it had always been her dad who had kept the dinner talk lively. Oh, how she missed him, even after all of these years. She couldn't remember ever seeing him without a smile on his face, a twinkle in his eye, and a newly heard joke on the tip of his tongue. Many were the times that he had soothed her young heart and unruffled her stiff feathers. If only she could pour out her soul to him now.

"Margie?" It was obvious that Grace had asked a question while Margie's mind had been wandering.

"Sorry, Mom. What did you say?"

"I just wondered if you'd like to do some shopping tomorrow. I need to pick up a few things and thought you and the girls might like to go along. We could have lunch and make a day of it." Then, turning to Leigh, "I don't suppose that would be much fun for you," she said. "Do you think you could occupy yourself here at the house for a day?" Leigh was agreeable; he had no desire to spend several hours in the company of four females indulging in retail therapy.

For the next three days, Margie's girls–actually young women now–spent the greatest portion of their time in and around the swimming pool in Grace's backyard, the rest of the time helping her with whatever task she was undertaking at the moment. Margie joined in on the projects, feeling almost like a child again.

On the evening of the reunion that had inspired their trip, Georgeanne and Cadence gladly stayed at home. The older daughter tuned in to her favorite television shows and sat glued to the screen, while Cadence had a hilarious time trying to better Grace at crazy eights. The older woman won every hand.

Leigh and Margie returned in the wee hours to find Georgeanne asleep on the couch and the other two still at the card table. Margie laughed delightedly when her daughter complained about her thwarted attempts at victory over Grace. "Don't you know that Grandma is the card shark of the family?" Margie explained.

"Oh, now, I wouldn't go that far!" objected Grace.

"Well, in all the years that we played cards, I don't remember anyone ever beating you!"

Grace chuckled and shrugged. "So are you ready to challenge the champion?"

"No, thanks, Mom. I know when I'm well off. I think we'll just call it a night–it is 2 am, you know! There was a time when you'd have had my head for staying up this late."

Grace chuckled. "Well, I don't have to worry any more about your immortal soul. It's all your responsibility now. I get to relax and just have fun, one of the perks of getting old."

The next morning they paid a visit to Margie's brother, dropped in for a few minutes at Aunt Leone's, then headed to Canoga Park to visit Richard's family. It had been seventeen years since they had seen each other, and Margie wondered if Richard had, in the interim, developed the pot belly and bald head that, sooner or later, seemed the fate of the entire male population. But when he opened the front door, Margie noted that he continued to sport a full head of hair–now touched with a few silver strands–and though he had become to some degree portly, he still cut a dashing figure in her eyes. In addition, he had maintained the ability to make her heart race and her body tremble. Linda, coming up behind him, was as beautiful as ever; was there no justice? Not only did she look fabulous, she had prepared a magnificent meal of prime rib, baked potatoes, two kinds of salad, and homemade rolls, with lemon meringue pie–not from Marie Callender's–for dessert.

"This is wonderful, Linda!" Margie exclaimed. "But we would have been happy with hamburgers or pizza, you know."

Linda shrugged. "I've always claimed that pizza is one of the more nutritious meals, since it contains all of the food groups except chocolate." They all laughed at this. "But I love to cook, so this was no trouble."

"Where's Gideon tonight?" asked Margie. "I was hoping to meet him."

"Oh, he's on an overnighter with some of the young men from church," explained Linda. "I'm disappointed, too, that he's not here. I kinda wanted to show him off. But he won't be back until late tomorrow night."

"Hmm. Unfortunately, we'll be gone by then."

Richard was uncommonly quiet during dinner, which caused Margie some uneasiness. Long lapses in the conversation made it evident that he was preoccupied, and Linda was struggling to find topics that would keep her company entertained. "Did Richard tell you he has a new calling at church?" she asked. "He's playing the piano for the Primary Organization."

Margie directed an amused look at Richard. "Are you liking that?"

"Best job in the church," he admitted with a grin.

"And do you keep the Primary children entertained the way you always did me?" she asked. Richard half-smiled, remembering their many long-ago evenings together at the piano.

"I've been told," remarked Linda, "that his prelude music is quite innovative."

Richard shrugged. "I have my moments."

Linda went on, "It seems that while the Primary presidency is scurrying around, getting things ready to begin, Richard plays his own version of 'skittering mice' music on the upper register of the piano." Margie grinned at Richard and Linda went on, "Last week, the bishop visited, and as soon as he stepped through the door, Richard began playing the theme music from *Jaws*." This tickled Margie; it was so characteristic of the Richard of her childhood.

Still, she couldn't shake the feeling of an underlying current that evening of . . . what? As she and Linda cleared the table and loaded the dishwasher, Margie inquired with some concern, "How's Richard's health? Is he okay?"

"Oh, yes. His heart attack was minor. He's getting along fine."

"How's Aunt Vera? Is she doing all right?"

"Oh, I think so. She doesn't say much. You know, she's never exactly been a fount of information."

Margie laughed. "None of the three sisters is! They all figure that their business is their business. In fact, I just barely found out that Richard was adopted!" Her hand flew to her mouth. She'd certainly had no intention of offering that particular tidbit of information. It was as if some unseen power had forced the disclosure from her lips.

Linda's eyes widened as she audibly gasped.

"You didn't know," stated Margie, becoming more and more vexed. Of course she didn't know. Richard had never been told!

"I don't think he knows," Linda countered.

Margie wanted to disappear–permanently. She immediately tried to backpedal. "Oh," she said, shaking her head, "I'm probably wrong. I must have misunderstood." She hurriedly turned to the sink, rinsed out the dishcloth, and began wiping the counters, hoping to avoid any further embarrassment.

But Linda remained thoughtful. "He has a birth certificate with his parents' names on it," she puzzled.

"Yeah." Margie waved her hand in an effort to dismiss her stupid blunder. "I'm sure I've made a mistake." But she could tell by the troubled expression on Linda's face that this would not be the end of it.

The Monroes returned to Bountiful, and a few weeks later, Margie received a phone call from Linda. Richard had invited his mother over for dinner the night before and, following their meal, had confronted her directly about the question of his birth. Margie was, once again, besieged with remorse. "Oh, my gosh, Linda, I'm so sorry! I don't know why I ever brought the subject up!"

"It's okay," replied Linda. "I'm pretty sure, judging by Vera's reaction, that you're right about it."

"Why? What did she say?"

"Oh, she denied it, of course, but the expression on her face told volumes. And usually when she comes to dinner, she stays and visits for awhile, but last night, she beat a hasty retreat. Said she had to get home, she had things to do."

"Oh, Linda, I could cut my tongue out!"

"No! Don't worry about it. Actually, I think Richard's relieved to know he's not related to some of your strange ancestors."

Margie laughed; she could appreciate the truth of that statement but was still heartsick over her terrible faux pas.

Chapter XXVII

Six months later, a disturbing letter arrived.

Dear Margie,

Sorry to have to lay some upsetting news on you. Linda and I have split up. We haven't been happy for some time. You may have noticed that things weren't great when you were here. It's nobody's fault–it just happened. We're still friends. She'll stay here in the house; I'm not sure yet what I'm going to do. I'll have to remain in the area because of work, so probably will just get an apartment somewhere. Gideon will live with Linda until he goes away to school. I don't worry about him because he's a good kid (even if he does play the bagpipes). I'll be in touch as soon as I'm settled somewhere so you'll have my address and phone number. Don't you fret about me, Kiddo. As I've told you before, I always land on my feet! Keep me in your happy thoughts!

Love,

Richard

Margie couldn't believe her eyes. Richard and Linda had seemed so right for each other. They'd had the same interests and the same goals, at least as far as Margie could tell. What could have gone wrong? No way to know until she could talk to Richard and, right now, she didn't even know where he was. Cooling her heels had never been Margie's forte.

It was two weeks before Richard telephoned. "Hey, Kiddo!" he greeted her.

"Richard! I've been going crazy waiting to hear from you! So tell me what happened. I thought you and Linda were happy together."

"Just one of those things, I guess. We had some good times, but things have pretty much been going downhill lately."

"But why? I don't understand! And don't tell me 'just one of those things'! There has to be a reason."

"Let's just say we're better off apart, and let it go at that. You really don't want to know. Trust me on that."

"Richard! Now I'm more baffled than ever." Margie paused as she considered the possibilities. "Oh," she said, realization dawning. "Maybe it's too personal. Sorry."

Richard laughed. "I doubt that anything you might be imagining at the moment is anywhere near the truth. You know that normally I would tell you anything you wanted to hear. And someday maybe I will, just not right now."

"Oh, Richard. You know it's going to eat away at me."

"Sorry, Kid. Actually, I called to let you know where I'm living and give you my phone number."

Margie got a pencil and jotted down the information.

Chapter XXVIII

The ringing of the telephone a few nights later brought Margie quickly, though reluctantly, to consciousness. She glanced at the clock on the nightstand by her bed: 1:20 a.m. A feeling of foreboding took hold of her senses. No one called at this hour except to relay bad news. With much trepidation, she lifted the receiver. An acerbic male voice on the other end of the line informed her that Gregg had been taken to the hospital, the result of a drug overdose.

"What?" Margie quickly sat up, her muzzy mind not quite able to wrap itself around the man's words.

"Mrs. Monroe, your son, Gregg, is at University Hospital. He's presently in ICU while we try to stabilize his condition." Then it seemed to dawn on the man that his disclosure might be something of a shock to Gregg's mother, and he continued more gently, "Sorry, I assumed that you were aware of his drug dependency."

Margie was all too cognizant of the fact that Gregg used drugs but had naively denied that his habit may have escalated into "dependency."

"No!" she stated. "I mean, yes, I knew he used drugs."

"You understand that he's presently unconscious. There's a

possibility that he may not wake up."

Margie gasped. "I'll be right there." She rigorously shook Leigh, who she had always claimed could sleep through an earthquake whose epicenter was in their living room. While she dressed herself, she explained to her torpid husband the plight of their son. "Do you want to go to the hospital with me?" she asked.

"Is Gregg okay?"

"No, Gregg isn't okay! He's unconscious! He's in ICU! He's addicted! How can he be okay?" Margie's panic lent sharpness to her response. "Do you want to come or not?"

Leigh swung his legs to the side of the bed while stifling a yawn. "Yeah, I'll go." He rubbed his face with his hands and ran his fingers through his hair, then scratched the back of his head and yawned again.

"You don't have to. I can take care of it."

"I said I'll go. Just give me a minute to wake up."

"I'll wait in the car. Hurry!" With that, she grabbed her purse and keys and left the room. She was frantic concerning Gregg's present condition, more than a little angry about his freewheeling choices, and livid over Leigh's blasé attitude.

Calming her hostilities, she quietly crept into the room shared by Cadence and Georgeanne and gently woke her younger daughter, apprised her of the situation, and asked that she keep an eye on her sister until they returned. Then she walked out to the car, climbed in behind the wheel, and waited. The minutes ticked slowly by, five and then ten, and still Leigh had not emerged. Margie's vexation was at an all-time high. She threw open the car door and ran furiously into the house. There in the bedroom lay Leigh, his feet still on the floor, his head on the pillow, his open mouth emitting raucous snores. Margie paused just long enough to assess the situation, then returned to the car and left. She was beyond trying to make Leigh into the caring, sensitive man that her heart longed for. From now on, she would just plan from the start to do everything on her own. Then she wouldn't continue to be disappointed.

Margie dreaded entering the hospital. It brought back too many unbearable memories. She stood for a moment outside of the building, took a deep breath, offered a silent prayer, and finally approached the formidable doors. She was directed to the small waiting area, where the doctor joined her and explained that Gregg's chances for a full recovery were good . . . this time. "Some of these kids fry their brains to the point that they never wake up. Your son is one of the lucky ones today, but if there's a next time..." He shrugged and shook his head. "Who knows?" The good doctor's anger was showing, and Margie couldn't blame him. Dealing with this kind of stupidity day in and day out could understandably make one testy. But the victims' parents shouldn't be the target of his wrath, should they?

After looking in on Gregg and receiving the doctor's assurance that there was no need for her to stay–Gregg would be out for some time yet–Margie returned home to sleep for a couple of hours before it was time to begin her day. Following what felt like a five-minute nap Margie took a shower, fixed breakfast for Leigh and the girls, and left Cadence in charge–fortunately it was a Saturday–while Leigh went to the office to catch up on some work, and she made her way back to the hospital.

She couldn't help but wish that Richard were here to offer his infallible comfort and advice. She had no doubt that he would know how to handle the situation, what to say to Gregg when he finally woke up, and how to dissipate former hostilities. Margie longed for a strong man to lean upon–someone who would be willing to share her burdens.

Gregg regained consciousness a day later and, after the social worker declared him to be no threat to himself or others, was discharged. Margie drove him straight to her house, turned off the car engine, and sat back against the seat, shoulders slumped. "You can stay here for a few days until you're ready to go back to work," she offered. "That is, if you still have a job."

"Thanks, Mom." Gregg was contrite. "I hope you know that I didn't do this on purpose."

Margie sighed. "How do you take drugs 'not on purpose,' Gregg?"

"I mean I wasn't trying to kill myself or anything. I would never do that. I just got careless."

"But don't you see, Gregg? You are killing yourself. As long as you keep doing what you're doing, that's the only possible outcome. I just don't understand why you would deliberately mess up your life like this."

"You're right; you don't understand."

Margie's temper flared. "So this is my fault?"

Gregg rolled his eyes. "No, I didn't say that. Not everything comes with blame attached, Mom. Some things just happen."

"So, why did this happen?"

"I told you, I got careless."

"I don't mean just this. I mean the whole thing. What got you started in the first place? Were you unhappy? Were you having problems we weren't aware of? What?"

"Not unhappy. Not happy. Maybe just bored. I dunno."

Margie swore that she would not lose control, but she was having a difficult time maintaining her objectivity. She took a deep breath. "You know," she finally said, forcing herself to inject a little lightness into the mood, "if everyone who was ever bored began a program of self-destruction, you never would have been born."

Gregg, for once, didn't misinterpret his mom's feeble attempt at humor and snorted softly.

"So, where do we go from here?" asked Margie.

"I dunno, Mom. If you want to know the truth, I'm really scared."

"About what, exactly?"

"The future, I guess. I know my life isn't worth much right now, and even though you may not believe it, I really want to change things. But I've heard stories about guys who go through rehab. I don't know if I could survive it. And yet, like you said, the alternative is going to kill me for sure. I guess I feel like I'm all out of options."

"And you may not believe this, but I understand that feeling all too well." She smiled at him. "You know that I'll do whatever I can to help you get through this."

"Yeah, Mom, I know that."

After a good deal of soul searching, Gregg finally entered, by his own choice, an outpatient rehabilitation program. Margie didn't have much confidence that this long-standing problem was finally on its way to a solution. There had been a time when nothing to her had seemed impossible, but life had taken its toll. It wasn't the great tragedies–she somehow managed to cope with them–it was the day-to-day disillusionments. Over the years, as her natural optimism had slowly seeped away, a new cynicism had crept in to take its place, and she despised the change in herself. If only she could once again become the Pollyanna of her youth. At this point, however, she was realistic enough to know that it was impossible.

But in spite of her lagging faith, she remained pessimistically hopeful of a recovery for Gregg.

The following months were marked by encouraging reports from Gregg's therapist, followed by devastating accounts of regression. Margie tried to adopt a "wait and see" approach but was defeated by her own passionate nature. Consequently, her emotions suffered irreparably from the constant reversals in Gregg's progress. At times, she felt so full of anxiety, she was sure that her head would explode.

Cadence was Margie's salvation–no concerns there. She was a good student, a dedicated musician, a blithe spirit. Margie wondered more than once how she had ever merited such a child. Somewhere in her distant past, she must have done something good. But if so, it was far enough back that she had no memory of it.

The situation with Georgeanne never changed, but at least Margie knew what to expect from her. She caused little turbulence but couldn't be trusted on her own. Margie often found money missing from her purse, and by the time the shortage was discovered, Georgeanne would have it spent. With a little ill-gotten cash in her pocket, she would ditch the afternoon school bus meant to bring her home and then hoof it into town. Leigh and Margie often cruised the city streets at night, hunting for their missing daughter.

Leigh's behavior also never changed. When Gregg abdicated from the family, the former outings with Dad came to an end, even for Cadence. With the exception of the occasional search for Georgeanne, the old routine of work, dinner, television, and bed was reestablished. Margie was too perplexed to care.

Eventually Gregg's treatment was terminated–the outcome was encouraging–and Margie almost dared to count her blessings. She knew that Gregg possessed the willpower to keep himself drug free now that the "drying out" period was at an end, if he would simply–or not so simply–exert the necessary effort.

Gregg began telephoning now and then, just to touch bases, and more than likely, to receive some needed support. His attitude toward the family was gradually changing. Things would never be the same as they had once been, but the new relationship was one that Margie could live with, perhaps even enjoy.

One tidbit of information was encouraging: Gregg was now taking a few classes at the community college in the evening and had hopes of eventually earning an associate's degree in design; he had inherited his father's talent for art.

During the next several months, Margie continued to worry over Gregg's stability. Even the slightest setback could be the end of his promising future. As each day passed without incident, Margie breathed a little easier. Then, one evening, the telephone rang. "Mom?" Gregg's salutation sounded tenuous and Margie's heart sank.

"Hi, Gregg," she answered cautiously, her brow furrowed. "What's up?"

"I've got some good news." This was so unexpected; it took Margie a minute to process it.

"Good news?"

"Well, I think it's good news. I hope you will, too."

Margie was still apprehensive. "What's going on?"

"Are you sitting down?"

"Gregg! Don't do that! What's your news?"

"Okay, I'm getting married."

Margie was thunderstruck. She and Leigh hadn't even known that he was dating anyone special. Not that Gregg needed their permission, but it would have been nice if he had taken them into his confidence a little sooner. Was Gregg jumping into a relationship that he would later regret? What about his drug problem? Would this girl be a good influence, or was she someone who would drag him back down? In spite of her reservations, Margie tried to put a smile into her voice. "That's quite a surprise, Gregg! So what's her name? When do we get to meet her?"

"It's Janet. I thought maybe the four of us could go out to dinner. Or, better yet, you could invite us over!"

Margie laughed conservatively. "I guess I could manage that. You want to come on Sunday?"

As the afternoon of their first meeting progressed, Margie became delighted with her soon-to-be daughter-in-law, and Georgeanne and Cadence were thrilled to be getting a new older sister. Janet was obviously a stabilizing force in Gregg's life. Being a couple of years his senior, she was already well established in her career and would be able to help financially while Gregg completed his schooling. Margie was gratified to note that they had obviously given much consideration to their future. Plans were ultimately made for a summer wedding, and Margie's heart was lifted at the prospect.

It would seem that Gregg was finally getting back on track, and Margie once again had hopes that he would find happiness and fulfillment. Margie wondered if Georgeanne could be so fortunate. It was apparent by now that she would never be self-sufficient enough to have her own home. Marriage was clearly out of the question, and Margie wondered what would become of her oldest daughter when she was no longer around to care for her. Would one of her siblings take her in, or would she be relegated to some kind of group home? Georgeanne's prospects weighed heavily on Margie's mind.

Cadence, on the other hand, held no fears for Margie. She was now in the eleventh grade, was accompanying the high school choir, marching with the drill team, and cheerleading at the basketball games. Margie loved all of her children, but Cadence was the brightest star in her sky. In addition to her many accomplishments, she was the kindest, most caring individual Margie had ever known. She was the one whose peers sought her out whenever they had a concern, academic or otherwise. The Monroe home usually hosted two or three of Cadence's friends each evening, working through an algebra problem, planning a party, or receiving "advice to the lovelorn." Thank goodness for Cadence.

Chapter XXIX

In July, Gregg and Janet were married, enjoyed a brief honeymoon at Lake Tahoe, and returned to Salt Lake to set up housekeeping. A week after their return, on a Thursday night, they received a call from Margie.

"Gregg?" Her voice was flat.

"What is it, Mom? What's wrong?"

Everything was wrong. She should be feeling something: devastation, fear, anguish, something! But there was nothing there; she was devoid of emotion. "It's your father," she finally said. "He's been in an accident and is in the hospital."

"Which hospital?"

"University."

"I'm on my way."

Gregg shared with Janet the shattering news, grabbed the keys from the hook in the kitchen, and ran out the door. Janet followed him to the car. "Do you want me to come with you?" she asked.

"No. I'm not sure how long I'll be." Gregg jumped into the car and started the motor. "I'll let you know as soon as I find out what's going on." He backed out of the driveway and sped toward the hospital, panicking over what he might find there.

Georgeanne and Cadence were occupying a small love seat against the far wall of their father's darkened room, their faces dour. Margie was seated in an armchair at the side of Leigh's bed, absorbed in her own thoughts. She was experiencing a strange sense of déjà vu. It didn't seem that long ago that she sat at Davey's bedside, praying for a miracle and even more recently at Gregg's.

She now gazed at her husband's battered body and reviewed in her mind their almost twenty-three years together. She recalled her long-ago telephone conversation with her mother when Grace had observed that Margie seemed to be "happy enough." Had she been? Had Leigh? Maybe no one is ever more than just happy enough. She knew she had wanted too much–from Leigh, from life! She had certainly experienced a good share of disappointment and heartache, but she suspected that her life had been more fulfilling than Leigh's. Was it Gloria Steinem who said that the tragedy is not to die but never to have lived? Had Leigh ever lived? Had he at any time experienced supreme elation–or even darkest despair–over anything? The only occasion that had ever elicited profound emotion was when he had dropped Davey. But, even then, his grief and guilt seemed to dissipate quickly. Though the many sorrows that Margie had endured had seemed unbearable, knowing nothing but tedium would have been worse.

"Mom?" Gregg's voice intruded on her reverie.

"Oh, Gregg." She stood and gave her tall son a hug. "Why don't you pull up that chair over there?"

Gregg crossed the room and quietly greeted his siblings. Cadence had her arm linked through Georgeanne's, her head resting on the older girl's shoulder. Georgeanne was, to all appearances, less traumatized by the day's events than her younger sister, and Gregg wondered for a moment what might be going through her mind. Did she understand, at all, the possible ramifications of their father's injuries? Probably not, and probably better so. He took hold of the empty chair and slid it to the side of Leigh's bed, the sound of its legs scraping across the floor irritating his already tightly strung nerves. He then sat down and asked, "What happened, Mom?"

Margie sighed. "He'd taken off early from work and was on his way home. A drunk driver ran a stop sign and broad-sided him. There's major head trauma, and even if he regains consciousness, chances are that he has lost his motor function and much of his mental faculties." She shook her head. "I can't believe that this is happening again."

"Isn't there something they can do?"

Margie shrugged. "He was in surgery all afternoon. They relieved the pressure on his brain. Now they say we just have to wait. Would you call your Grandma Grace when you get home and let her know what's going on? I didn't phone any-one but you."

"Okay. Do they have any idea how long Dad will be out of it?"

Margie shook her head. "No. But the longer he's in a co-ma, the less chance of him ever coming to. Hopefully, by to-morrow, we'll know more."

"Do you want me to stay with you?"

Margie appreciated the offer, would have liked his compa-ny, but refused, thinking of his new bride waiting at home. "You don't have to do that. I'll call you in the morning."

Gregg stood, walked around the bed, and leaned over to kiss Margie on the forehead. "Okay, Mom. Try to get some rest. What about the girls? Do you want me to take them home?" But they both shook their heads in silence. Gregg hugged each of them and lifted his hand to Margie. “I’ll see you tomorrow then.”

Margie dozed on and off in the chair, always disoriented upon awakening until she remembered where she was and what had brought her there. In the morning, nothing had changed. It was ironic that Leigh and Davey had suffered such similar injuries, and Margie searched her soul for the strength to go through it again.

A nurse, who was just coming on duty, entered and began taking Leigh’s vital signs and registering them on his chart. Looking up at Margie she observed, “You look like you could use a good cup of coffee. Would you like me to get some for you?”

Margie smiled. “No, thanks, but I would like to go home and shower. Is it safe for me to leave him for that long?”

“I don’t think anything’s going to happen in the next hour or so, Hon, but we’ll call if there’s any change.”

Margie gathered her daughters, who had spent an uncomfortable night on the shared love seat, and they drove home. The phone was ringing as they entered the front door, and Cadence ran to answer it.

“Hello.” A pause. “Oh, hi, Richard. Yeah, she’s right here.” Then, turning to Margie, “Mom, it’s Richard.”

Margie had felt no tendency toward tears until she heard Richard’s voice. Then the floodgates opened. “He’s not doing well at all. He’s still in a coma, and they don’t know how extensive the brain damage is, but they suspect the worst.”

“I’m coming up there.”

“No, no,” Margie declined. “There’s nothing you can do. We’re just waiting to see what happens. It might be a long haul; they just don’t know. There’s no reason for you to come all that way.”

"On the contrary, dear cousin, it's what I want to do, and that's reason enough. I'll need to clear up a couple of things at work, then I'll hop the next plane. They owe me some time off, so it won't be a problem. Should be there tomorrow sometime. Where will I find you?"

Margie realized that arguing the point would be fruitless, and in reality, she longed for Richard's comforting presence more than anything else she could think of. Just seeing him would do wonders for her flagging spirit, so she not unwillingly conceded. "I'll probably be with Leigh, but come here to the house. Cadence can show you the way to the hospital."

They said their good-byes, and Margie turned to her daughters. "Why don't you girls get some sleep? You don't need to go back with me."

"But what if something happens?" worried Cadence.

"I'll call you right away. Go get some rest." With that, Margie headed for a quick shower and then returned to the hospital. She was functioning by robotic impulses, performing the expected routine, while her heart and mind lambasted her with guilt. She should have been a better wife, less self-centered, more forgiving. She'd tried, spasmodically, each time resolving to do better, with each resolution subsequently eclipsed by some infuriating action of Leigh's. Then she'd allowed her resultant annoyance to become exacerbated, first by the sheer accumulation of offenses, and secondly by her own never-ending regrets. In short, she had made a shambles of her life.

The next afternoon, Richard rented a car at the Salt Lake Airport and drove to the Monroe home. A teary-eyed Cadence answered the door and ushered him into the living room, summoned her mother, then disappeared up the stairs. As Margie beheld her cousin standing there, something inside her perceptibly collapsed. Richard stepped forward and drew her into his arms.

"Richard," Margie murmured, "Leigh died this morning."

"Oh, Margie, I'm so sorry. You've had more than your share."

Margie pulled away, grabbed a Kleenex from her pocket, and dried her leaking eyes, her tears more a lament over the fact that she had miserably failed in her marriage than from the grief that a normal wife should be feeling. She motioned for Richard to have a seat on the couch, then curled up beside him and leaned her head against his chest as he put his arm around her shoulders.

"He never regained consciousness," she said. "I guess it's probably a blessing; he wouldn't have been the same."

"What about you?" Richard questioned. "Are you okay?"

Margie nodded. "I just wish I'd done better by him." She began to sob again. "He was a good person, just insensitive and immature. I should have been able to overlook his failings and appreciate him for his better qualities."

Richard stroked her hair with his free hand, making her feel like a cherished child again. "You're taking too much credit," he remarked sarcastically.

"The worst part," Margie began, then thought better of it. "Never mind."

"The worst part?" Richard urged.

Margie shook her head. "Nothing."

Richard took her by the shoulders and forced her to look at him. "The worst part?" he insisted.

"The worst part is that I don't feel anything. That scares me, Richard. What kind of an insensitive monster am I?"

Richard sighed and leaned back again. "I'm no psychologist, but my guess is that you've been mourning Leigh for years, probably for the whole time you've been married. Now there's just nothing left. Does that make any sense?"

"Maybe; at least it makes me feel better."

"Okay, then, let's just forget the self-recriminations for now and concentrate on getting you through the next few days."

Margie relaxed against the cushions. "I'm so glad you're here, Richard."

He smiled at her tenderly. "So what do you need me to do?" Richard, as usual, was stepping easily into his role as her self-appointed caretaker. "Are you okay financially? Do you need some cash to carry you over?"

"No. I'm fine. The one good thing about Leigh selling insurance for that short time is that he set up a good policy on himself. And, because it was an accident, the amount is doubled, so I won't have to worry about money."

"Mm. What about food? Do I need to go to the store?"

Margie smiled at the thought of Richard grocery shopping. Surely he must take care of his own; she had just never envisioned him doing anything as mundane as pushing a grocery cart. "Actually, the women from church have already brought in dinner for tonight. And I think they're planning on taking care of meals for the next few days."

"Well, then," Richard paused, trying to judge the state of Margie's emotions. "Will you be all right for a little while? I didn't take time to check into the hotel, so maybe I should go and do that; then I'll help you get things sorted out around here."

Margie sat up. "Don't be silly. There's plenty of room here at the house. You're not going to stay at a hotel!"

"But what will the neighbors say?" he halfheartedly joked.

Margie laughed in spite of herself. "I always have liked to

give people something to wonder about. So, no more discussion, I'll show you where to put your bags. You'd just as well turn in the rental car, too. You really won't need it while you're here."

It was late when Margie and Richard finally turned off the last light and said goodnight. Richard climbed the stairs, and Margie retired to the room she had shared with Leigh for so many years. She changed into her pajamas but somehow couldn't bring herself to crawl into the bed where her husband had slept, so she grabbed a blanket and pillow and carried them to the couch in the living room. After an hour of tossing from left side to right and back again, she gave up all hope of sleeping that night and went to sit on the front porch. The air was beginning to cool, and Margie welcomed the relief from the stuffy house. She walked out onto the lawn, relishing the feel of it on her bare feet and basking in the vastness of the night sky overhead.

Richard, meanwhile, had turned on his bed lamp, pulled a book from his suitcase, stacked the pillows against the headboard behind him, and was attempting to read. He knew this would be a long night. After laboring over the same paragraph three times, he laid the book aside, got up, and went to the window. Leaning on the sill, he glanced below and discovered Margie in the middle of the front yard, staring up at the stars. She was humming to herself, and the sound ascended through the night air to fill him with nostalgia. The corners of his mouth involuntarily curled upward as he observed her still figure. She then turned and walked toward the house, pausing long enough to pick a daisy from the bush by the side of the porch. She lifted it to her nose and inhaled deeply, then placed it over one ear. Suddenly changing directions, she tentatively turned on one foot, making a full circle. Then, gaining momentum as she went, she pirouetted across the front lawn, finally collapsing in quiet giggles on the grass.

Richard descended the stairs and walked through the open front door onto the porch and down the steps. "Is this a private party, or can anyone come?" he asked, startling Margie, who was sitting cross-legged on the ground, intent on plucking up patches of grass.

Her head jerked up and she smiled. "You couldn't sleep either?" she asked.

Richard shook his head as he approached her.

"You want to sit with me on the porch for awhile?" Margie offered.

He smiled. "I'd rather watch you do some more of your little twirling thing out here on the lawn."

Margie's eyes widened. "You saw that?" Richard merely grinned. "Now I'm embarrassed."

"Not at all," Richard assured her. "I thought it was charming."

Margie guffawed as she stood and moved toward the house, Richard following. "I was reliving my youth," she explained. "I used to like to see how many pirouettes I could do without getting dizzy. I was never very good at it, and I definitely haven't improved with age." She settled herself on the top step and patted the spot beside her, then folded her arms and rested them across her knees. Richard obediently sat down and mimicked her posture. "We used to have some fun times, didn't we, Richard?"

"I hate to sound like an old fogey," he said, "but 'those were the days.'"

"What about the days since then?" Margie asked solemnly. "How good have they been for you?"

"I'm just like anyone else, Margie. Some good times and

some bad."

"And how do you survive the bad?"

"Huh," Richard huffed. "Look who's asking whom. You've had to deal with a lot more than I have. How have you survived?"

Margie turned toward Richard and leaned back against the stair railing. "What choice have I had? There have been lots of times when I wanted to cease existing. Just be dead–I mean really dead. Without any awareness. But, since there is no way to annihilate the soul, I've had to survive; there were no alternatives."

"Have you never been happy, Margie? I don't mean when you were a kid. I know you were happy then." Richard emitted something between a chuckle and a grunt at the memories this evoked. "Ah, yes, you were my little ray of sunshine. But what about since then?"

"That's the second time today that you've called me 'Margie.' I don't want to be 'Margie' any more. I just want to be 'Kiddo.'"

Richard reached over and took her hand. "You'll always be 'Kiddo,'" he assured her, "but tonight I want to hear about 'Margie.' What is she thinking about?"

"I guess I'm just looking for answers. I'll admit that some of the things that have happened to me I have brought on myself through my own bad choices, as you well know." She smiled at him ruefully. "Other bad things have come because of someone else's choices. But I don't count any of those because someone has been at fault, either myself or, usually, one of my children. But there are other things that happen to us over which we have no control and no one to blame. Those are the things I'm trying to understand. What I want to know is, first of all, why was Georgeanne born with a damaged brain? She is one of the sweetest people I know. She never gets upset, and she's kind and thoughtful. She just doesn't deserve the hand she's been dealt. And Davey. Why did he have to die? I can't even find the words to describe Davey. He was my angel child."

"We're never going to have all the answers, Margie, not in this life–oh, I mean Kiddo." Margie chuckled. "But it sounds to me like Davey and Georgeanne were, and are, too perfect to be subjected to all the stuff you and I have to deal with.

"But you haven't really answered my question. In spite of all the heartaches, hasn't there been something that has brought you happiness?"

"Of course there has, lots of things. I'm just wallowing to-night."

"What about from here on out? What exactly do you want out of life?"

"World peace," Margie answered.

Richard laughed. "You sometimes make it very difficult to carry on a serious conversation."

"Sorry. It's just that, at this point, I find it hard to think about the future."

Richard pulled Margie beside him and laid his arm across her shoulders. "Do you remember the first time I told you about the stars?"

"I remember it all, Richard. Everything you taught me, every song you ever played for me, every touch, every tender glance. I even remember you scolding me for going to a certain party one night . . . everything. You filled my world."

"Then why . . . " Richard shook his head. "Never mind. No point in hashing over the past."

"Why did I mess everything up? I wish I knew. At the time, I thought I was doing the right thing. But now, even if we were blood related, it just doesn't seem that important any more." In a lighter tone, she asked, "Do you suppose that I might possibly be finally getting my priorities in order?"

"We live in hope, Kiddo."

Margie backhanded him across the chest and Richard laughed. "I see you haven't lost your backswing."

"I can't afford to with you around."

"I like being around," Richard admitted softly.

Margie didn't answer. She was suddenly reminded of the reason that Richard was there and felt guilty that she had, for the last little while, forgotten. "The sun's going to be coming up soon. We probably should try to get some sleep."

"You're right," admitted Richard as he stood, pulling Margie up with him. "Tomorrow will be a long day." He led her inside and to the bottom of the stairs, turned and cupped her chin in his palm. He gazed into her eyes, then looked down at her lips, tempted–oh, so tempted.

Margie sensed his inclination and backed away slightly, offering a quiet, "G'night, Richard."

He smiled and placed his lips softly on her forehead. "Night, Kiddo."

Richard was a great consolation to Margie throughout the next few days, taking charge in his own inimitable way, helping her make a thousand decisions, and then following through with their execution. He stayed until Leigh had been laid to rest, and for a week afterward, whether to comfort Margie or merely satisfy his own need to be with her, he couldn't say. Whatever his reasons, Margie was overcome with gratitude for his stalwart presence. She basked in his loving care, always pleasantly aware of his nearness, and consequently badgered by guilt. She had, after all, just buried her husband.

The dreaded time finally came for Margie to drive him to the airport, and after checking Richard's bag and obtaining his boarding pass, they walked together down the concourse to the waiting area by the gate, where they located a couple of adjacent chairs. As they sat down to wait, Richard leaned forward in his seat, resting his elbows on his knees. He gazed at the floor and fidgeted, something obviously on his mind.

Finally, he sat back and cleared his throat. Margie gave him a questioning look, but he pretended not to notice. She smiled at his uncharacteristic reserve. "Yes?" she prodded.

Richard turned his attention to her, gauging his approach. "It's probably none of my business, but since you're obviously beating yourself up over what you perceive to be multiple flaws in your character, I have to ask. What happened between you and Leigh that made things go wrong?"

Margie choked, nonplused, but Richard obviously expected an answer. She looked away from him. "You did," she muttered. "Leigh did the best he could, I think. He never caroused, never chased other women, never spent money foolishly . . . and never failed to disappoint me."

"I'm not sure I follow."

Margie sighed. "I always expect too much of everyone, but I especially expected it from him. I constantly compared him to you." She smiled. "Pretty hard to compete with perfection." Richard chortled softly as she went on. "And I'm also not the easiest person to live with; I know that."

"Well, as I've told you before, you're a strong woman," noted Richard.

Margie uttered a soft snigger. "Or maybe I'm just ornery. It's possible to confuse the two."

"I've known you all your life and never seen an ornery side. Of course, I haven't had to live with you for the last twenty years either," Richard joked. "Have you gotten mean in your old age?"

Margie pretended to be affronted. "Old age? C'mon, Richard. We're not old, just mature, or seasoned maybe. But never 'old.'"

Richard lifted his eyebrows. "Speak for yourself. You seem to forget that I have a few years on you, Kid."

"Well, when you reach our age–or, rather, maturity–the difference is negligible."

Richard nodded. "I have to admit, being here with you, I can almost believe I'm still a young Lothario."

Margie guffawed. "Lothario? Is there something about your deep dark past that you haven't told me?"

"Shweetheart," Richard curled his upper lip, creating his best Bogart impersonation, "you'd be surprised!"

As the PA system crackled to life, announcing his flight, Richard stood and pulled Margie to her feet, keeping hold of her hands as he faced her, his former lightheartedness rapidly disappearing. He once again cleared his throat and shook his head. "All kidding aside," he paused. "I worry about you being on your own. You may be strong, but you're not indestructible." Richard was indecisive about continuing. "Ah, what the heck! I know this isn't the best time to bring it up, but I just want you to know that I'm still here. When you get tired of being alone. Well, I think you know what I'm trying to say."

Margie half smiled and tilted her head to one side. "Oh, Richard, if you were anyone else, I'd probably smack you in the face!"

Richard grinned, almost blushed, and cast his eyes over her right shoulder. "Sorry, Kid." He shook his head and looked back at Margie. "But just keep it in mind. Meanwhile, I'll stay in touch." He placed a kiss on her cheek, turned, and walked through the door to the boarding ramp.

Margie watched him disappear, plunging her heart into despair, and wondered how she would survive. Richard had always been there for her, no matter the cost to himself, and she had never missed him more than she did right now. She turned away, a tightness in her throat as tears blurred her vision.

Chapter XXX

Margie took her time driving home; she was in no hurry to arrive anywhere, least of all back to a houseful of memories. As she stepped through her front door, she was assailed by a palpable void. Though Leigh had never been a masterful presence in their lives, his irrevocable absence nevertheless bombarded her senses. While Richard was there and they were busy with all of the activity surrounding Leigh's death, she'd had little time to notice. It had seemed, somehow, that he was still with them. But now the vacancy was conspicuous and strange. Georgeanne was in the living room, watching television, and looked up as her mother entered. "Hi, Mom."

"Hi, Sweetie." Margie sat wearily on the sofa next to her daughter, feeling the inevitable letdown that invariably follows such an eruption in one's life. "Where's Cadence?" she asked.

"She's in the kitchen, talking to one of her girlfriends on the phone."

Margie smiled. Life goes on, it would seem. "How about going out to dinner tonight?" she asked. "I don't feel much like cooking."

Cadence appeared in the doorway, having overheard Margie's comment. "Mom," she said, "you don't ever feel like cooking! But, yeah. Let's get dressed up and go splurge at a really expensive restaurant. We need a night out."

"How about the Hotel Utah?" suggested Margie. The girls happily concurred and quickly changed into appropriate dress.

Their dinner conversation that night centered on memories of Leigh, and Margie was gratified to notice that Cadence was able to recall many pleasant occasions in company with her father.

"Remember when we all went ice skating on the pond that time? I think I was about six. None of us had ever been on skates before, but Daddy was the one who fell and broke off his front tooth–and he just got up and went on skating! He was having too much fun and didn't want to quit." Cadence was quiet for a moment, then began to chuckle. "I'll never forget the time we took a picnic up the canyon, and Daddy started a water fight. By the time it was over, we were all in the middle of the stream, totally drenched and still throwing water on each other." Again she retreated into her own thoughts. These were happy memories for Margie as well, and she appreciated being reminded of the good times.

"One thing I regret," Cadence continued, suddenly becoming somber, "is that I could never get Daddy to draw a picture of me." She smiled ruefully at Margie, her eyes glistening. "Why wouldn't he do that for me?" she asked plaintively.

Margie smiled with understanding. "He had his reasons. He didn't do serious portraits, only caricatures, and he only did men. Said that women were too easily offended. I don't know about that, but nevertheless, it was his hard and fast rule, even where his own family was concerned. He wouldn't do one of me either."

Cadence was appeased and continued with several more

recollections as Georgeanne sat quietly listening, having little to contribute. Margie studied her older daughter's features, looking for some hint of jealousy but found none. Her brow was clear and she was smiling, obviously captivated by Cadence's anecdotes. Margie wanted to weep as she compared the relationship between Cadence and her father with that of Georgeanne and the same father. She was certain that Leigh had never intentionally favored one daughter over the other, but Georgeanne was easily disregarded, whereas Cadence was difficult to ignore. It wasn't hard to understand why Leigh might have excluded his older daughter from the outings with his other children; she did, unfortunately, require extra attention and care. But it broke a mother's heart to see one of her babies slighted, through no fault of her own, and especially by her own father.

Margie's own memories were mixed and therefore kept to herself. There had been happy times, certainly, but she had allowed them to be overshadowed by the fact that her innate desire to be cherished and protected had never been fulfilled. She didn't blame Leigh; she knew that she had always desired, nay demanded, more from him than he was able to give. No, she accepted full responsibility; she had recognized, right from the start, his deficiency in the traits she so highly esteemed and settled for less than what she wanted. As her daddy used to say, "We're too soon old and too late smart!"

The morning after their extravagant dinner, Margie knew that she must tackle the unpleasant task of going through Leigh's personal belongings and determining how to dispose of them. His clothes wouldn't fit anyone she knew and so could simply be dropped off at Deseret Industries Thrift Store. Perhaps that was the best solution for all but what the children might want to keep as mementos. Still, it was a daunting undertaking. As she pulled each item of clothing from its hanger, she recalled the occasions when she'd seen Leigh dressed in that particular shirt or jacket, and she felt somehow cheated that more of her memories weren't happy ones.

It took her the better part of a week to gather and fill the number of cardboard boxes needed to accommodate Leigh's accumulations, and she breathed a sigh of relief when the project was completed. Gregg came over on Saturday to give her a hand, and the girls helped as much as they could. But it was Margie who had to make the final decisions about whether to give or throw away.

And then there was the question of what to do with Margie herself. Cadence was quite self-sufficient for a seventeen year old, and in addition, led a busy social life, which left her minimal time at home. She had her driver's license and was responsible behind the wheel, so Margie was comfortable with allowing her to provide her own transportation. There was really nothing for which she needed her mother. And while it was true that Georgeanne required more care than would a normal child (even though she was an adult physically, in many ways, she would always be a child), Margie foresaw endless hours hanging heavily on her hands.

She'd long had the desire to write, but the time had never before seemed propitious. Would that she had accomplished the deed while her daddy was still with them; a good spine-tingling mystery would have pleased him no end. She chuckled at the thought. Still, better late than never; but perhaps a love story would be more within the scope of her abilities.

The telephone interrupted her ruminations, and she was abundantly pleased to find Richard on the other end of the line.

"Just checking up on you," he said. "Are you doing okay?"

"I'm fine. I've just been wondering what to do with the rest of my life. I'm suddenly at loose ends. I've always wanted to write a book. What do you think?"

"I'll be the first in line to buy it."

Margie laughed. "Well, I'll let you know if it ever becomes a reality. What do you do to keep busy?"

"Oh, I'm playing in a dance band and still directing community theater. Why don't you begin a career in acting?"

Margie guffawed. "Am I not a little too old to take Hollywood by storm?"

"Now, wait a minute," Richard retorted. "Weren't you the one who was telling me that we're not old, just mature? Besides, I wasn't exactly thinking Hollywood. That might be a mite ambitious. But community theater is always looking for 'mature' actors."

Margie wished that she could consider such a fulfilling activity. "That would be tempting, but I'm afraid Georgeanne keeps me pretty much tied down."

"Then I think a novel is a good idea. And while you're waiting for your creative juices to flow, why don't you come down for a visit?"

"A very appealing suggestion," Margie granted, "but you seem to forget that I still have a daughter in school."

"I haven't forgotten, but I was thinking maybe Christmas vacation."

Margie mulled over the idea. It would be nice to get away for awhile, perhaps gain a new perspective on her future. And, of course, see Richard–her stomach hatched butterflies at the prospect. "I'll give it some thought," she promised.

Chapter XXXI

As the holidays approached, Margie was having second thoughts about traveling. California was an enticing proposition, but she balked at the idea of driving there in December; a good deal of snow and ice-covered road stretched between Bountiful and warm weather. She hadn't even considered the possibility of flying–old penny-pinching habits died hard. If not for Cadence suggesting an airplane trip as an alternative, she may have discarded the idea of a winter vacation altogether.

With their flight booked, they eagerly packed enough clothes to last the duration of their junket and, as soon as Cadence's classes were out for the holidays, the three of them were on their way–full of exuberance. Margie couldn't help feeling a bit nervous, however, as she anticipated the reunion with Richard. True, it had only been a few months since Richard's visit, but Margie had, at that time, still felt like a married woman, and Richard had behaved accordingly. So, would they now fall back into the old easiness with one another, or would their new circumstances–both of them single, available . . . and unrelated–make for an uncomfortable awareness that would stifle the spontaneity they had once enjoyed? Since there was nothing she could do but wait and see, Margie leaned back and tried to relax for the duration of the flight.

Grace picked them up at the LA Airport and, with all of the excited chatter that ensued, the few miles to her home were covered before they knew it. This trip had been a wonderful idea, and Margie silently blessed Richard for the recommendation. It was emotionally soothing to become Grace's "little girl" again, a phenomenon which occurred without fail whenever Margie stepped foot inside her childhood home.

Richard telephoned soon after they arrived. He understood that Margie would need to spend a day or so with Grace before he could see her, but he was anxious to set up a meeting. Margie, though slightly apprehensive, was also eagerly looking forward to seeing her cousin. She couldn't help but wonder what was in store for the two of them. Would it be possible for them to recapture the carefree mood of their youth? Or did they now carry too much baggage? She was almost afraid to find out.

For three days, the women shopped, lunched out, took in a couple of movies, and generally laughed and played together. All of the years of hardship, guilt, and disappointment melted into oblivion, leaving Margie feeling like a new woman. Nevertheless, it was the same familiar image that she beheld as she stood in front of the mirror getting ready for her evening with Richard. She had managed to maintain her high school weight but hadn't been happy with it in high school either.

"I'm considering a body transplant," she announced to Cadence, who had just come in to check on her mom's preparations. "Just have them lift the hair and replace everything from there down." She grimaced. "On second thought, why save the hair?"

Cadence laughed. "Don't be so hard on yourself, Mom."

"Does this dress make me look frumpy?" Margie inquired. "I probably should have colored my hair before we came. Are these shoes all right?"

"Calm down, Mom. You look fine," admonished Cadence. "After all, it's just Richard!"

Margie lifted her eyebrows at her daughter. Just Richard? Richard had never been "just" anything.

He arrived exactly on time, as usual, and, also as usual, had planned an elegant night out. The restaurant was swank–linen tablecloths and dimly lit crystal chandeliers, the waiters decked out in tails with a napkin draped over one arm–and provided a small dance floor with a band specializing in music from the forties and fifties. The evening brought back exquisite memories of former lighthearted days and ended up at the location of so many of their happiest hours. The roar of the ocean was balm to Margie's soul.

Richard turned off the car, leaned back against the seat, and pulled Margie close to his side as they watched the moonbeams dancing on the surf. "Seems almost like old times, doesn't it?" he observed. "Think there are any cops on patrol, shining their flashlights into parked cars, the way they did in the old days?"

"And have you had experience with that sort of thing?" Margie asked in mock astonishment.

"Not me!" Richard exclaimed vehemently. "My friends used to tell me about it." He chuckled. "Can you imagine how surprised a cop would be if he were to catch a couple our age making out in the back seat?"

Margie was amused at the thought. "Is that what you have in mind, Richard? A little making out?" she teased flirtatiously.

"The thought had crossed my mind."

Margie chuckled softly, in no way opposed to the idea. "And what would our children say?"

"What children?" he facetiously inquired. With that he drew her closer and planted a kiss soundly on her lips.

Margie was left breathless, her head spinning. "We didn't do that in the old days," she sighed.

Richard raised one eyebrow. "We did a couple of times," he reminded her.

Margie smiled in sweet remembrance of that first sweet kiss on a long ago New Year's Eve. "Yes, but not like that."

Richard nodded. "More's the pity. I wanted to often enough."

Margie was intrigued. "So what held you back? I never considered you to be the shy type."

"I'm not sure. I think maybe I was scared."

"Of me?" Margie asked, incredulous.

"Yes, of you. You have no idea, Kiddo, of the effect you had on me. Besides, you were so confoundedly innocent, I felt like I had to protect you from everything, even me." He gave a slight chortle. "Maybe most of all me."

"Forever the gentleman," Margie observed. "I was glad you were; it made me feel safe. But we're not exactly the same people that we were back then."

Richard drew back, feigning affront. "You mean I'm not a gentleman anymore?"

Margie laughed. "Well, you did kiss me just now."

"Hmm," he nodded. "Okay, so other than the fact that I've turned into a cad, what's different about us?"

"Besides the crow's feet, you mean?" Margie joked.

Richard regarded her with amusement. "On you, my dear, even crow's feet look good!"

Margie pulled away and backhanded him on the chest, refusing to acknowledge the compliment that secretly pleased her. "You're supposed to deny that I have them!" she complained.

"Oh boy," he huffed. "I guess I'm way out of practice at charming the ladies. But back to my question. How else are we different than we used to be?"

Margie paused, timid about introducing the one subject they had never before discussed. "Well, there is the thing about us not being cousins anymore," she said softly.

"Ah, yes!" Richard concurred. "There is that. Not that it ever mattered to me."

Margie was penitent. "If only I'd known," she lamented.

"Water under the bridge, Kiddo. Let's forget about what might have been and just go on from here." Then in a lighter tone, "What else is different?"

"Well," chuckled Margie, "I'm not so innocent anymore."

Richard shouted, "Hallelujah!" which made them both laugh. "And what else?"

Margie pondered for a moment. "Oh, I think you're not quite as carefree as you used to be," she observed.

"Hmm. You're probably right. But I know how to fix that."

"Oh?" Margie drew back and raised her eyebrows. "Have you discovered the Fountain of Youth?"

"Mmm," Richard shrugged, "in a manner of speaking." Margie gave him a puzzled look, then leaned her head back against his chest and waited for him to go on. "You make me feel young, Kiddo. I'd like to talk you into sticking around for the duration."

Margie sighed. "Oh, Richard, I don't think you understand what you'd be taking on. You know Georgeanne's going to always be with me. She'll never be able to fend for herself. And I won't put her into a home as long as I'm capable of taking care of her. You don't realize what a burden that could be."

Richard pulled Margie away from him and turned to face her squarely. "My dear, sweet, stupid cousin. All my life I have longed to take care of you. That means sharing your burdens and lightening your load. If I could, I'd take all of it, so that you'd never have another moment of grief for the rest of your life. If I can help you with Georgeanne, that's frosting on the cake."

"But, what if - "

He cut off her objections with a tender kiss. "Let me worry about the 'what ifs.' Just say yes. Please?"

Margie saw the devotion in Richard's eyes and wondered if she dared give him the answer that he was seeking–the answer she, herself, had always wanted to give.

She looked down at her hands. "It's not only Georgeanne," she continued. "I'm just really afraid."

"Why?!" Richard couldn't imagine that Margie would still have reservations.

"I don't know. What is it they say about getting married? Why ruin a beautiful friendship? How can we be sure that won't happen?"

Richard shook his head in frustration. "Do you love me?" he asked almost peevishly.

"All my life," Margie admitted, looking deeply into his eyes.

"Then isn't it worth taking the chance?"

Margie leaned her head against Richard's shoulder, overcome with the love she felt for him and no longer capable of denying herself one last chance for happiness. "Yes," she acquiesced. "I guess maybe it is."

Richard folded her into his arms and breathed a sigh of relief. It had been a long, hard battle, but he had won. They had both won.

Chapter XXXII

As soon as Margie and her daughters returned home to Bountiful, they immediately began preparations for the small wedding she and Richard had planned. She felt like an eighteen-year-old again as, with her girls in tow, she scoured the whole of Salt Lake City searching for the perfect dress, simple but elegant, probably in a pale peach, if she could find it. Georgeanne and Cadence were willing participants; as Margie modeled, they judged each creation, sometimes with wrinkled brows and grimaces, other times with unrestrained giggles, with their mother initially feigning offense, then gleefully joining in. At long last, Margie found the dress she had been looking for: a lined sheath of crêpe de Chine which hit her midcalf, with a matching midriff-length jacket embroidered just below the shoulder with a delicate floral pattern. Her daughters' expressive faces when she paraded before them corroborated the rightness of her choice.

Margie was giddy with happiness, filled to the brim and overflowing with love for Richard, and experiencing a sense of freedom she hadn't enjoyed since she was fourteen. The girls applauded their mother's high spirits; they had never seen her so happy.

Their future home would be in California, close to Richard's employment, and Margie was delighted to be returning to her beloved birthplace. Nevertheless, she had mixed emotions as she contacted a real estate agent and placed the Monroe house on the market; her heart held tender feelings for the home she'd leave behind. Each room contained a fond memory of one of her children. There at the kitchen table, was where she was sitting paying bills the day Gregg burst through the front door with his first straight A report card. She could still remember the wide grin on his face, the light in his eyes, and the feel of his arms around her neck as she enfolded him in a congratulatory hug. And this was the room Cadence decorated as a surprise for her parents' twentieth wedding anniversary. Gregg was, by then, well on his way down the thorny path to self-destruction, and Margie was in the dark days of her depression. She had taken Georgeanne to see the doctor for a sinus infection, and when she returned home, was greeted with crêpe paper streamers and a lopsided wedding cake. She remembered bursting into tears, which clearly distressed Cadence, until her mother explained that her tears were the result of her daughter's thoughtful kindness, rather than from sorrow or disapproval. And here was where she and Georgeanne had spent so many happy hours reading the little girl's favorite books, or perhaps they were Margie's favorites: *Cinderella* and *Black Beauty*, with the *Wizard of Oz* at the top of the list. A new home would hold no such connection to the past, but Margie was willing to exchange her ties to yesteryear for the promise of a bright future with the only man to whom she had ever completely surrendered her heart.

Margie intended to sell most of her furniture–it made more sense than trying to move it all–and placed an ad in the newspaper, which garnered some immediate responses. She and her girls then began the seemingly endless process of packing everything they would take with them. There was plenty to do before school was out for the summer, with the wedding date so closely following.

Georgeanne, of course, had no problem with the idea of moving; wherever Mom was, it was home for her. Cadence, on the other hand, was experiencing an emotional upheaval. This was her senior year in high school, and she and her friends had been classmates and chums for a long time. They were looking forward to their last summer together and one "final hurrah" before many of them would enter various universities in the fall.

Margie could relate to her sorrow, recalling her own last summer at home before entering college. It seemed now like another lifetime with another Margie. Undoubtedly it was. Today's Margie was, hopefully, a better person than the one now being dredged up from the past. She smiled to herself. That had been a wonderful lighthearted summer, in spite of the occasional bursts of–not anger, really, just vexation–between Wade and her. Those were memorable days, and Margie was filled with remorse over the sacrifice that Cadence would be making. There just didn't seem any way to avoid it; Richard's work schedule for the next several months was immutable.

"It's okay, Mom," Cadence assured her. "It can't be helped. And you deserve to be happy." Margie, not for the first time, acknowledged that her youngest daughter was an exception to every rule. Where had such a selfless, sensitive spirit come from? It had always been Cadence who had soothed her troubled spirit with words of comfort and encouragement, forever exhibiting maturity beyond her years. Margie suspected that the child had fully recognized the difficulties between her parents, though she had never mentioned the fact. But during those times when Margie was reprimanding herself for her own inadequacies, Cadence was forgiving them both with demonstrative compassion.

Margie made arrangements with Grace for the girls to stay with her during the honeymoon, and finally it seemed that everything was taken care of other than loading up for the trip west. The house still hadn't sold, but Margie felt her agent to be trustworthy and was confident that she would fairly represent the family's interests.

Richard had, meanwhile, purchased a home for them in Thousand Oaks and had already moved in. "I even bought a lawn swing for the front porch," he announced to Margie over the phone, "so we can sit together on long summer evenings and reminisce. We'll split the time between the porch and the piano," he promised, making her laugh. It all sounded too good to be true. She found it hard to believe that this could really be happening, that she and Richard would actually be spending the rest of their years together, never again to be separated. The thought made her heart race; she had never been so happy.

At 11:00 pm on the night before their planned departure, the telephone rang. Margie had not yet retired; she was too keyed up to relax, so was sitting in an armchair reading. She picked up the phone from the table beside her and, expecting to hear Richard's voice on the line, answered with a cheerful "hello."

"Margie?" The voice was very like Richard's but not his. "This is Richard's son, Gideon," he explained.

"Oh, Gideon, I've heard so much about you. It's too bad we've never met. But that will soon be rectified. You'll surely be at the wedding?"

There was a pause on the other end of the line. "That's what I called about." He hesitated. "I'm sorry, Margie." His voice broke.

"What?" Margie's face fell–she couldn't imagine that Richard had changed his mind. "What's wrong?" she asked in panic, her spine involuntarily straightening.

"Dad had another heart attack tonight. I'm afraid it's bad news."

Margie's head began to swirl. "What do you mean?" she demanded. "Is he going to be all right?"

Gideon was finding it difficult to proceed. "He . . . he didn't make it."

Margie shook her head in denial. "No!" This couldn't be happening! It was all some incredible error.

Gideon continued, "I'm sorry to be the one to tell you. I don't know what to say. Mom's here to help me get everything taken care of. I'll call you back tomorrow after we get some things figured out. I'm really sorry."

Margie sat with the receiver in her lap, her body limp. "Richard, you can't leave me!" she cried. "Not now. It's not fair!" She could almost hear his voice reminding her that, "Life's not fair, Kiddo." She slumped back in the chair and let the tears fall. She was tired. Tired of being strong, tired of being lonely, tired of being disappointed, tired of having her heart broken . . . tired of living.

Cadence appeared in the doorway, still awake, finishing up her packing. "Mom, I can't decide - Mom? Are you okay?"

Margie turned an anguished face to her youngest daughter. "No."

Cadence walked slowly to her mother's chair and knelt by her side. "What happened?"

Margie relayed the grievous news in between sobs, barely

able to get the words out.

"Oh, Mom, I'm so sorry."

Margie shook her head bitterly. "Not as sorry as I am." She took a deep breath. "I don't know when the funeral will be. Gideon will call back tomorrow. Just pack a small bag and help Georgeanne put something together; I think we'll fly down. No use taking all our stuff until we figure out for sure what we want to do."

On what was supposed to be her wedding day, Margie tearfully viewed the lifeless body of her beloved Richard. Linda was standing by the casket, greeting the mourners, while Aunt Vera sat in a chair close by. Margie couldn't help feeling a stab of jealousy; she should be the one receiving condolences. On the other hand, she was grateful that Linda had stepped in and overseen the funeral arrangements. Gideon was really just a kid; it would have been difficult for him to manage it alone. And, in all honesty, she supposed that Linda had the right. She had, after all, been Richard's only wife.

Margie steeled herself as she approached the casket. Linda, the ever-gracious lady, embraced her warmly and whispered, "I can't tell you how sorry I am that things turned out this way." She then took a step back, still grasping Margie's arms. "It's just not fair, is it?"

Margie slowly shook her head as she reluctantly moved her gaze to the still form beside them. "Richard always told me that life isn't fair. But this . . . this exceeds all bounds." She reached her hand toward the casket and ran her fingers along the back of those familiar musician's hands, remembering how they used to move over the ivories, producing the tones that spoke to Margie's soul.

Tearfully, she turned back to Linda and suddenly remembered to introduce her daughters. It was then that she noticed the tall young man at Linda's side. He took Margie's breath away. There stood Richard, some thirty-odd years ago. Margie reached out to him, and he grasped her hands. "Gideon," she sighed, gazing intently at his all too familiar face. "You're so much like your father!" She couldn't keep from staring; the likeness was uncanny. "I'm Margie, by the way."

Gideon nodded. "I know. Dad showed me your picture. Over and over again!" He smiled. "I've never seen him happier." The lump in Margie's throat prevented a response, so she merely nodded and gave him a hug. She then spoke briefly with Aunt Vera before she and her girls moved into the chapel where they joined Jack and Grace, who had driven up from Westchester for the services. Aunt Leone's family had evidently not yet arrived.

The funeral was unlike any other that she had ever attended. Could "joyful" be used to describe such a solemn occasion? The eulogy, read by Gideon, portrayed a man so full of mischief, so rich in talent, so bigger than life, one wondered if he could possibly have been real. Richard's droll sense of humor was extolled by all who spoke, as they related numerous hilarious anecdotes, moving the congregation first to laughter and then to tears. Margie, herself, could not hold back her mirth over recounted incidents that were so completely Richard-esque. Finally, some of his original compositions were performed by a small group of his fellow band members. This was music that Margie had never before heard, a glaring reminder of the many of Richard's accomplishments to which she had not been privy and causing her to further lament the years that the two of them had spent apart. Her tears erupted and rolled unrestrained down her cheeks, as sobs involuntarily burst forth from within. Cadence placed her arm around her mother's shoulders, but even Margie's most compassionate child could not soothe her battered heart.

Following the proceedings at the graveside, Gideon approached Margie. "I wondered if you'd like to go with me to Dad's house. Well, I guess it's your house now. I found an envelope addressed to you there on his desk. I left it where it was, but I assume he would want you to have it."

Margie informed Grace of their intentions, assuring her that they would see her later that evening, and she and her daughters climbed into their rental car and followed Gideon to a beautiful, two-story white stucco house on a quiet cul-de-sac. It looked to be about fifteen years old, with three mature sycamore trees adorning the front lawn. Pansies lined a flagstone walk leading to the wide front porch, where sat the lawn swing to which Richard had referred.

Gideon opened the door, revealing a wide entry with a large sunken living room to the right and, facing them, a gracefully curved stairway leading to the second floor balcony. As Margie stepped inside, she caught a faint whiff of Richard's cologne and, for a moment, expected to see him suddenly appear from another room. Then reality intruded once again, sending a sudden jolt through her being as she reached into her bag for a tissue to staunch the ensuing flow. Would this wretched weeping never stop?

Margie could also see a formal dining room through French doors on her left. "What a beautiful home," she dolorously observed, surveying the elegance surrounding her.

"The study's in there." Gideon indicated a door to the right of the stairs. "I'll be out in back if you need anything."

Georgeanne settled herself on the sofa in the living room and picked up Richard's old photo album from the coffee table–that would keep her occupied for some time–while Cadence accompanied Gideon on a tour of the back yard. Margie entered the study, definitely a man's domain–undeniably Richard's. She located the envelope with her name scrawled in a familiar hand on the outside, hesitantly pulled out the single sheet from within, and sank down into the plush desk chair to begin reading.

To my soon-to-be blushing bride (or don't you blush any more, since you've lost your innocence and all?),

I guess it's a little strange for me to be writing when we'll see each other in just a few days. But I was sitting here thinking of you and felt the need to record my thoughts, just in case I forget.

The anticipation of our "I do's" is almost more than I can handle. They've been a long time coming. We didn't turn out to be an old maid and an old bachelor, did we? Just "old." Sorry! I mean mature!

Margie smiled ruefully and continued on.

When did that come about? Whatever happened to that curly-headed little blonde who used to climb up beside me on the piano bench and listen to whatever nonsense I coaxed out of the ivories? Is she still buried somewhere inside the beautiful woman you have become? I picture us in the future, side by side on that piano bench, spending happy hours together the way we used to do. You had me twisted around your little finger at that very young age, and soon you were twisted around my heart.

I've never told you the reason for the breakup of my marriage. Maybe now's a good time–reveal all my deep, dark secrets. Linda, poor girl, got tired of playing second fiddle (so to speak). Much as I tried to be a good husband to her, she was never fooled. She knew my heart had always and would always belong to you. Pretty hard for anyone to live with that.

A wave of remorse swept over Margie–so much unhappiness, all because of her. She'd accumulated enough should and shouldn't haves to last three lifetimes.

I've been trying to remember when I first started loving you (as more than my cousin, I mean). I think it may have been that night when you came to see me in the hospital after I had my appendix removed, and you laid your head on the side of my bed and cried. I wanted to pick you up and hold you next to my heart and never let you go.

I still want that–to hold on to you forever. If you were here, I'd sing to you (even though you'd probably laugh the way you always did when I sang) that song that Gene Kelly croons in "An American in Paris," when he tells Leslie Caron about all of the things in life which are merely passing fancies, such as the radio and the telephone and the movies. Even the Rocky Mountains and the Rock of Gibraltar are transitory when compared with their love.

The same goes for ours, Kiddo; it's here to stay!

Keep me in your happy thoughts.

Richard

Margie leaned back, unaccountably comforted by Richard's final declaration of his undying love. She stood and walked to the window that looked out over the back lawn. There she caught sight of Gideon and Cadence side by side on a wicker love seat, deep in conversation. She still couldn't get over the startling resemblance that young man bore to his father, both in looks and mannerisms. And she had to admit that

Cadence was her mother's daughter. Watching the two young people was almost like seeing herself and Richard thirty years ago. If only it were. If only she could roll back the calendar and start over, doing things the right way this time. If only she had known the truth sooner. So many "if onlys." She turned back to the desk, sat, and picked up pen and paper.

My dearest Richard,

I wish you could sing to me now; I can promise you I wouldn't laugh, except maybe for pure joy.

I've been looking out the window, watching our children (so much like we used to be) getting acquainted, and I'm reliving sweet memories of bygone years. Do you suppose he's telling her about the stars or maybe philosophizing about the eternities? Perhaps they're discussing music or books. Does Gideon know everything about everything the way his father did? You might laugh at that, but to me you were the quintessential sage.

Now you've left me and my heart is broken. You are my hero, my guide, my protector, my everything. You've always been there for me, even when we were miles apart.

Now we're worlds apart! Is our love strong enough to cross the veil between? Will you still be around when I need you? Are you here now, when I need you most? Can our devotion withstand this separation? Will we have eternity to make up for lost time?

I'll be loving you always,

"Kiddo"

Margie left the note on the desk, stood slowly, and strolled through the house, torturing herself by imagining what her life might have been here with Richard. The sunny kitchen where they'd have discussed over breakfast their plans for the day, Richard always having something in mind that would surprise and delight her; the dining room where they'd have entertained their friends and family, with Richard's endless stories and observations evoking joyous laughter; the fireplace, before which they'd have snuggled together on cold winter nights, perhaps with a good book that they were sharing. She could easily picture them growing old (older, she ruefully admitted) together in this house. They were in the autumn of their lives; winter could have been beautiful, warmed by the glow of Richard's love. She stood at his piano and brushed her fingers over the keys, wishing that she could once again hear it speak to her the way it had so many times under Richard's strong and gifted hands. "Oh, Richard," she moaned, "how can I survive without you?"

Margie returned to the entryway, opened the front door, and walked out onto the porch. The sun was just setting. She turned and slowly approached the swing, hesitating for a moment before sitting down against its soft cushions. Margie put the swing in motion and watched as the sky began to darken. Twilight, a beautiful word. Her favorite time of day. A slight breeze was riffling the leaves on the sycamores, and in the house next door, a light flicked on. Margie winced slightly, her solitude disturbed. Through the open window, she could hear what sounded like a bench being slid on a hardwood floor. There was then a squeak and a scrape as the unwitting intruder was seated, followed by a thunk. Someone struck a few basic chords and then began to play, while singing in a rich baritone:

Days may not be fair
Always;

That's when I'll be there
Always-
Not for just an hour,
Not for just a day,
Not for just a year,
But always.

Margie closed her eyes and sighed, "Thank you, Richard."

Acknowledgments

I couldn't have done it without the following people:

My daughter Tami, who kept me in line concerning the medical aspects of the book, and also completed the first proof reading.

My granddaughter Natalie, who forced me to reach beyond myself.

My Tap Dancing Buddies, Gay and Juanita, who did the final manuscript read through before submission, and who, along with Janet, Joyce, Rama, and Vicki keep my spirit dancing, though we've woefully been forced to hang up our tap shoes.

My publishers, American Book Publishing, who were willing to take a chance on me. I am forever grateful.

My editor, Amie McCracken, who has a tremendous sense of what works, as well as a very meticulous mind. She has held my hand through this whole process. I can't say enough.

My lifelong friend Vaudis, who accepts no excuses, but continually prods me along with, "You can do this!"

My earthly children, Jake, Gwen, Tami, Lonnie, Mikal, Tim, Natalie, and Angela, who have taught me everything I know about life, and have always responded to my literary efforts with enthusiasm.

My heavenly children, Lisa and Jared, who tutored me in some tough lessons while they were here on earth, and who I believe are, even now, cheering me on.

About the Author

Nannette Monson Kern was born in southern California and spent her first seventeen years playing on the beach (except when school interrupted). She then enrolled at Brigham Young University as a music major with a minor in English and a focus on extracurricular activities. She married during her junior year and returned to California to settle into married life and begin raising a family (her number one priority).

Following the birth of her third child, she and her husband moved their small household back to the Rocky Mountains, where they subsequently added seven more children to their family.

Finally, after thirty years of diapers and tricycles, she resumed her education, this time at the University of Utah, where she graduated summa cum laude with a B.S. in psychology. She has always loved to write, but until now, has shared her endeavors only with family and friends. This is her first novel.